Also by Philip Pullman

The Ruby in the Smoke

Shadow in the North

The Tiger in the Well

Spring-Heeled Jack

The Broken Bridge

the white mercedes

BY PHILIP PULLMAN

Alfred A. Knopf  New York

Library of Congress Cataloging-in-Publication Data

Pullman, Philip
The White Mercedes / by Philip Pullman.
p.   cm.
Summary: Seventeen-year-old Chris, living and working in Oxford, falls in love with an elusive girl
and while searching for her discovers the devastating consequences of placing his trust in the wrong
person.
ISBN 0-679-83198-3 (trade)—ISBN 0-679-93198-8 (lib. bdg.)
[1. Mystery and detective stories. 2. Interpersonal relations—Fiction. 3. Revenge—Fiction. 4.
Criminals—Fiction. 5. Oxford (England)—Fiction.] I. Title
P27.P968Wh   1993
[Fic]—dc20   92-11072

Manufactured in the United States of America
10 9 8 7 6 5 4 3 2 1

PART ONE

one

Chris Marshall met the girl he was going to kill on a warm night in early June, when one of the colleges in Oxford was holding its summer ball. The undergraduates were having their final fling before leaving to become merchant bankers or diplomats or advertising agents. They paid a great deal of money for tickets to balls like this—a hundred pounds, or even more in some cases. For that they expected a great deal in return, and the organizing committees worked hard to provide it: marquees with dance floors, champagne buffets, hot new bands and famous old ones, alternative cabarets—whatever entertainment was fashionable, expensive, and available.

This particular college had grounds that bordered a lake. There were going to be fireworks, there was a 1920s-style dance band on a floating platform, there was a cabaret-circus in a marquee; it was altogether a spectacular event, one which the undergraduates felt embodied the wealth and splendor due to them, at this time, in this country.

Chris Marshall wasn't an undergraduate. He was seventeen, with a year still to go at school, and this was a holiday job of sorts, though the holiday was some way off yet. He worked part-time for a firm called Oxford Entertainment Systems, owned by a man named Barry Miller. Barry knew that Chris was saving for a decent bike, so he offered him twenty-five pounds for the night's work, even though he didn't really need help. Chris was glad to do it. He was tired of sitting at home with his mother and her new lover, trying to make conversation and feeling himself in the way all the time. He'd never felt like that at home before, and it was uncomfortable.

So on a warm evening in June, Chris found himself setting up the lights for the cabaret-circus: uncoiling lengths of cable, strapping them to upright stands with insulating tape, swarming up scaffolding to check the angle of a spotlight, plugging various cables into a dimmer board, replacing a fuse that had burned out, freeing a revolving color wheel that had become caught, and setting up the flashpans to make flashes of green fire, while Barry Miller talked cheerfully to the director of the cabaret.

Barry was a mild, energetic man in his late thirties, blond and lean and slightly shortsighted, which made him blink and open his eyes wide with what looked like innocent candor. Finally the director, twitching anxiously, went backstage, and Barry turned to see how Chris was getting on.

"How's it going?" he said. "Got enough powder? Blimey, there's too much in there. You don't need much powder for a socking great bang."

Chris spooned some fire powder out of the flashpans. These were fireclay dishes across the base of which was fastened fuse wire between two terminals. Some powder— green, red, or white—was put on top of that, and when the current was switched through, the fuse wire burned out, setting off a big flash. Chris hadn't used one before and hadn't known how much powder to put in.

"Have we got a script?" Chris asked.

"No. He's going to give me a nod from back there. I says does he want a cue light, but it's one more thing for him to fuss over and forget. I tell you one thing, this lot won't make it professionally. Bloody shambles. I mean, they didn't even want to rehearse the lighting cues. Shit, I mean, how careless can you get?"

The performance was due to start at half past midnight. Before that a jazz quartet would be playing in the marquee, followed by a gay comedian whose TV show had been taken off the air. Chris was bemused.

"I thought people came to a ball to dance?" he said to Barry. "There's so much going on, it's like a fair. I'm surprised they haven't got Dodg'em cars."

"Not a bad idea. I done dozens of these, Chris. This is a bit more ambitious, but I like that. Look, I won't be needing you till half past twelve. Go and have a wander. Mingle. Circulate."

"I'm not dressed for that," said Chris, but he did as Barry

said, fascinated by the braying voices of the young men, the bare shoulders of the young women in their ball gowns, and the sheer beauty of the college grounds in the summer twilight, with torches flickering on the grass, lights glowing among the great trees, and the first snatches of music drifting over the water.

He'd lived all his life in Oxford, but there was a lot of it he'd never seen. The colleges were private places, except when tourists thronged them—bunches of bored Italian kids or interested Japanese adults—and Chris had no desire to mingle with them. Chris's Oxford was rougher, louder, dirtier than all that tourist stuff. It was the Jericho Tavern, where good, new independent rock bands came to play; it was the football stadium; it was the Speedway, where Chris had gone every week till he tired of it and began to cycle seriously instead.

That was his Oxford, not this upper-class fairyland. Chris decided then and there that whichever university he went to, it wouldn't be the one in his native city. For one thing, he didn't like feeling looked down on, and he was conscious of the faintly curious looks he was getting, casually dressed as he was in jeans and a T-shirt, plainly neither a guest nor a waiter.

In fact, he looked as if he might have been a member of a rock band. He was good-looking enough, with rough dark blond hair, and fit and muscular from his cycling. He looked older than he was, and if a person's character shows in their face, Chris's face showed independence and openness and courage. It might have showed innocence, too.

When the night was completely dark and the ball was fully under way, Chris wandered down to the edge of the lake. There was a little boathouse under some great dark trees at the far end, and he wanted to see whether there was a boat in it. He left the floating bandstand, with its jokily suited orchestra and brilliantined, megaphone-holding singer, and made his way into the green darkness under the trees.

The air was scented with the heavy sweetness of flowers from the college garden, and with the perfume of girls, and with the warm, slightly rotten smell of the vegetation at the edge of the water. Chris moved more slowly and finally stopped altogether at the corner of the boathouse, not quite sure why he'd stopped, not quite sure of anything but intoxicated by something.

He stood looking back across the water, watching the dancers on the wooden floor by the bandstand swaying to the music of "Blue Moon." From this distance they looked not offensively upper-class but tiny, glamorous figures, handsome men in black and white, and beautiful girls in colored gowns, like some old-fashioned dream of elegance and grace.

They looked even more striking because of the vast darkness that surrounded them, as if they were the last people left at the death of the universe and they knew it, but they were dancing anyway because they were human and because the best way of being courageous was, at that

7

moment, to dance. The distant words came over the water and Chris stood there entranced while the old song unwound, while the saxophone wailed like a ghost, while the dancers swayed. He knew he'd remember this moment for the rest of his life.

Then he turned away from the boathouse to go back, but he stopped because there were footsteps coming along the path. Someone was running toward him. The darkness among the shrubs and bushes was intense, but there was a glimmer, and there suddenly appeared before him a terrified girl in a white ball gown.

Her dark eyes were wide; her delicate shoulders were trembling. She cast a glance over her shoulder, and he heard stumbling feet and male laughter from a little way back. The line of her throat in the faint light from across the lake was enough, on its own, to make him fall in love.

"Someone chasing you?" he said quietly.

She nodded. Short dark hair, bare slender arms, those wide terrified eyes. . .he was lost.

"Go around there, in the boathouse," he said. "I'll keep them away."

She darted past, so close that he could smell the scent she was wearing. She vanished around the corner. He stood in the path, waiting for her pursuers, perfectly at ease, perfectly confident.

Within a few seconds they were there, and then they saw him and stopped: three young men in dinner jackets and black bow ties, one clutching a champagne bottle, another smoking a cigar, all drunk.

"Look, Piers," said one. "She's changed into a *chap*."

"Do him anyway," said another, lurching forward a step, but the third held him back. He was the one named Piers, and Chris could see that he was fair-haired and handsome.

"Who the hell are you?" he said.

"Not dressed properly," said the one with the cigar.

"Chuck him in the pond," said the one with the bottle. "I would."

"I'm a lighting technician," said Chris. "I'm checking the lights down here. That's who the hell I am. Okay?"

"There aren't any lights down here."

"They're not on yet, are they?"

The three of them stood there uncertainly.

"Well, anyway. . ." said the cigar smoker. "Anyway, if you're a technician, you ought to keep out of sight, I reckon. You don't pay a hundred pounds to see a lot of bloody workers slouching about."

"Where's Jenny?" said the handsome one suddenly. "Have you seen a girl coming this way?"

"No."

"Bloody liar," said the champagne drinker. "She couldn't have gone anywhere else. You must have seen her."

"Don't tell me what I must have seen. I'm doing a job here. I haven't got time to waste talking to people like you," Chris said. He was ready to fight them if he had to, and they must have seen it, because they began to move away.

"Cocky little sod, isn't he?" said the one named Piers, the handsome one.

"Oh, shut up, Piers, for Christ's sake. Look, you, technician chap, we're looking for a girl in a white dress. She's—"

One of the others plucked at his sleeve and whispered.

He went on: "She's not well. She's had a spot too much to drink. She could hurt herself. You sure you haven't seen her?"

"Perfectly sure. I heard her, though."

"I thought you said—"

"I said I hadn't seen her," said Chris. "I heard someone running a minute before you turned up. Along the path, that way." He pointed away, along the edge of the lake. "And she didn't sound drunk—she sounded frightened."

"Yes, well, she's not quite, you know. . ." Piers tapped his forehead. One of the others snuffled with laughter.

Chris stood perfectly still. After another moment or two, the three young men began to move on.

"Bloody rude, you know. We *should* have chucked him in the pond."

"I'm *sure* there weren't going to be any lights down here. . ."

"They should either keep out of sight or be dressed like servants."

"Stupid little bitch. If she's gone and. . ."

The rest of the conversation was swallowed by the bushes and the darkness.

When he was sure they'd gone, Chris moved along the side of the boathouse to the front. It was a small place, big enough to contain two punts, perhaps, with a narrow wooden walkway around the inside.

He stood in the entrance and looked in. It was very dark, but he could see the glimmer of her white dress at the end. It looked as if she were seated on the planking.

"It's all right, they've gone," he said softly.

She said nothing. Thinking she might not have heard, he moved toward her. He remembered what one of the young men had called her.

"Jenny? Is that your name?"

Still no reply. He stood still, halfway along the side of the boathouse, peering closely to see if she was all right. Had she fainted? They'd said that she was not well, that she'd had too much to drink. She hadn't seemed like that in the few seconds he'd seen her, and when she'd brushed past he'd smelled her beautiful scent, not drink. But could she be ill?

He was perturbed now.

"Jenny? Are you all right?"

He stepped on the planks at the end of the boathouse, and with a faint rustle of fabric she fell forward, slowly. It was horrible. She was headless. He nearly cried out in terror, but then realized that it wasn't her: it was the dress. She wasn't in it. She wasn't in the boathouse at all.

He stood trembling, waiting for his heart to stop thudding, and then stooped and picked up the dress, crushing the stiff fabric to his face, breathing in the scent he remembered. Then he put it down gently and looked around.

He was full of apprehension. The first fear of horrible death was replaced by another: *Was* she mad, as Piers had implied? Had she taken the dress off in order to slip into the water and drown?

She certainly wasn't in either of the punts. The wooden bottoms gleamed faintly under the sheen of an inch or so of water. And she wasn't in the lake, as far as he could tell— though if she was under the punts or tangled in weed, he wouldn't have known.

Now what should he do? Raise the alarm?

Yes, of course, and right away.

But no sooner had he begun to move than he saw what he'd missed a minute earlier. There was a door in the far wall of the boathouse. She wasn't necessarily in the lake after all.

A step or two, and he had opened it. The hinges were oiled; he and the three pursuers wouldn't have heard if she'd opened it and crept away. He stood outside among the tangled bushes and paused, uncertain. It had somehow become comic now, like blindman's buff. If she wasn't drowned under the dark water, she was hiding in the dark bushes without her dress. But why take it off? Because it showed up clearly in the gloom, and it rustled. It made sense.

He didn't know what to do. If he raised the alarm, it might be embarrassing for her.

"Thanks," whispered a voice from the dark.

Then he jumped, so much that he banged his elbow on the edge of the door. There was a giggle.

"Where are you?" he said.

"Never mind. Have they gone?"

"Yeah. I think. D'you want me to go back with you in case they're hanging around?"

"No. I'm not going back."

"Oh. . ."

Her voice was low and soft, and her accent was northern. It was the most expressive sound he'd ever heard.

"Why were they after you?" he said into the silence.

"Why d'you think?"

"You don't mean. . . Look, where *are* you? I can't talk to you like this."

"You're doing all right. But you're going to have to go now."

"Can't I help you?"

"You have."

"But they might come back!"

Silence.

"Jenny?"

Silence.

"Jenny, my name's Chris. Where do you live?"

Nothing. A silence as if she'd never been there. In the distance the band was playing another song, and somewhere in the green depths of the college grounds a nightingale was singing, but Jenny was invisible and silent. Had he

13

dreamed her voice? No, for he wouldn't have dreamed that Yorkshire accent, and he would have dreamed an answer.

So she was real. And alive. And it was—in the dim light, he peered at his watch—twenty past twelve.

"I've got to go and work," he said to the emptiness. Then, self-conscious but knowing that he'd be untrue to everything that had happened if he didn't put the feelings into words, he said, "Jenny, you're beautiful. I hope I see you again. If I don't, I'll never forget you, I promise."

Then he stepped away from the boathouse and felt his way through the thick bushes until he found the path again. He looked back and saw only meaningless shadows, patches of silver, patches of black. She might have been anywhere or nowhere; close enough to kiss or so far away that she'd heard nothing of what he'd said.

The dancers on their little square of light were clapping. The band struck up another tune, and the words came clearly over the still water, singing of moonlight, and trouble, and love.

two

Chris's parents had been living apart for a year, and in the month before the college ball took place they were finally divorced. Chris hated it far more than he could ever have guessed he would, far more than friends in the same situation seemed to; even worse than the betrayal was the calm, matter-of-fact way both his mother and his father now talked about it, as if the family had never mattered much in any case.

Chris had stayed with his mother in their large, comfortable house in North Oxford, while his father went to live with his girlfriend Diane, an ex-secretary from his architectural practice, in a small house on the other side of the city. Chris had been there a few times. The first time, Diane had been at home, and although he knew her from his father's office he found it difficult to talk to her, and he could see that she found it difficult too. She was pretty and a lot younger than his father, and to know that she was sleeping with his father and having sex with him made it confusing to look at her. And to look at his father, come to that. The next time he'd gone she hadn't been there. He'd asked, "How's Diane?" and his father had said, "Oh, fine, thanks," and they'd both been cool and adult about the whole thing. But talking wasn't easy for a while. It had been before, when they were a family, but in those days talking hadn't been an end in itself; it had just happened naturally.

As for his mother, at first she'd been grief-stricken. She was inclined to dramatize things anyway, Chris thought, to exaggerate and pose, but it couldn't have been easy for her to think about what his father was doing. She'd cried bitterly and locked herself in the bedroom a lot of the time, and when she came out she'd be brittle-cheerful and drink more wine than she used to. And her friends would come and see her more often and stay longer.

Chris had had to change. In a day, almost, he'd had to change from someone who was too young to drink or smoke or swear, even, into a sort of sympathetic brother who would listen wisely and give shrewd advice; someone who could talk about sex and lovers and mistresses without getting confused and embarrassed. He seemed to be expected not to want his father there, not to want his parents to love each other—to have grown out of all that.

And shortly afterward his mother began to see a lot of a man named Mike Fairfax, who was a university teacher and a city councilor, keen on liberal politics and environmentalism and the problems of the Third World. She took up with his friends and started going to meetings and wearing badges. And one night Mike Fairfax stayed and slept with her. The next morning they were elaborately casual, but Mike couldn't help looking sheepish. Chris's father had many weaknesses, but he was never sheepish.

So Chris wasn't happy at home, and when the summer holidays came along he spent a lot of time out of the house. It helped that he was working for Barry Miller's Oxford Entertainment Systems; but mainly it helped to have Jenny to look for.

Not a day went by without his thinking of her. She filled his dreams; she lay with him in his thoughts; he went to sleep and woke up with her name on his lips. She was with him all the time, and he had no idea how to find her, but he kept searching. And there was always the job to enjoy.

Oxford Entertainment Systems had two addresses. There was the warehouse off the Cowley Road, where most of the equipment was kept and repaired, and there was a shop nearer the city center, where small items could be rented or bought and where orders could be placed for the hire of larger pieces such as stage blocks or blackout curtains or lighting trees. Chris was one of four employees: Sandra worked in the shop, Dave and Tony at the warehouse and on the van, delivering or collecting materials for hire. Chris was to spend time in both places, repairing lamps in the warehouse, or packing the van, or checking returned equipment; or in the shop selling theatrical blood or make-up or wigs, or hiring out props such as Roman helmets or automatic pistols.

It wasn't really a seasonal job. Barry Miller said he'd be happy to take Chris on permanently, and Chris wouldn't have minded; but he knew that his future didn't lie in working for Barry Miller, agreeable as that was, so he regarded this job as a holiday from the real world and decided to enjoy it. After all, it was through the job that he'd met Jenny.

And it was because of the job that he found her again. On the first Wednesday of the school holiday he'd spent the morning in the warehouse, and now it was his lunch hour, after which he was going to spend the afternoon in the shop, learning the ropes from Sandra. He was cycling down the Cowley Road, past the betting shops, the Asian groceries, the newsdealers, and the trade union offices, when he saw Jenny coming out of a supermarket.

He nearly fell off his bike. She was on the other side of the road, and she'd turned down a side street, but the part of his brain that was now tuned permanently to slender girls with short dark hair had registered her in the corner of his vision, and he was sure it was her.

As soon as the traffic was clear, he darted across the road and down the street she'd taken, a place of little terraced houses with a brick chapel on the corner. She was just turning through a gate: a slender figure in a green T-shirt and black cycling shorts, carrying a shopping bag.

He slammed the bike into low gear and got there just as she was putting a key in the door.

"Jenny!"

She stopped and turned. No doubt! It was Jenny, and in this dusty sunlight she was no less beautiful.

"Who are you?" she said.

"Chris. The other night—at the ball. Remember? By the boathouse?"

"Oh. . .oh, yeah. Right!"

And she smiled. Chris's heart turned over. She was real, and she was here.

"Is this where you live?"

"Yeah. For the time being. It's a squat."

It was his turn to say "Oh. . ."

She opened the door.

"Want to come in?"

"Yeah. Thanks."

Bare floorboards, posters tacked to the walls, the smell of burned toast—it was a long way from the moonlit romance of the lakeside, and suddenly Chris was shy.

She led him through to the little narrow kitchen. Two young men were sitting at the table drinking coffee. They certainly weren't Piers and his friends; both of them had matted hair in imitation dreadlocks, imitation because they both were white, and they wore filthy, oil-stained jeans. One wore nothing above his waist, and was being tattooed on the shoulder by the other, with a pin and a bottle of ink.

"This is Chris," she announced. "Derek and Ollie. You want some coffee?"

"Oh, thanks, yeah."

19

Derek and Ollie seemed friendly enough. Derek, who was being tattooed, moved up to make room, and wiped his shoulder with a dirty handkerchief.

"Can you hold that mirror for me?" he said to Chris, who held up the little plastic-framed glass for him to check the progress of the tattoo. It was going to be a rose, though the mess of blood and ink made it difficult for Chris to be sure.

"It's always best to have assistance when it comes to tattoos," Derek explained. "I knew this bloke once who had the letters M-O-T on his forehead. Thing was, his name was Tom, and he'd done it himself in the mirror. All right, Ol, carry on."

"He must've been disappointed when he realized," said Chris, watching Jenny turn on the gas under the kettle.

"Take the shine off your whole morning, wouldn't it?" said Derek. "He went bananas. I've never seen anyone in such a rage. But it was too late. Fate had marked him out. At first he refused to answer when people called him Mot, but he had to in the end, or else have no one to talk to. Sad business."

"Do you all live here?" Chris said.

"Yeah. For the time being," said Derek. He seemed to be the talkative one, or perhaps Ollie was just concentrating. Jenny was rinsing some mugs in the sink.

"Who owns it?"

"Who knows?"

"But are you just living here rent-free? How did you find it?"

"Broke in. It's been empty for months. No, we don't pay

any rent, but we keep it cleaned and repaired and looked after. I suppose eventually we'll get kicked out, but there you are, *c'est la vie*. We're beneficial parasites. We live in a symbiotic relationship with our host, you see. We each benefit. It's dead ecological."

"Yeah, right," said Chris. He supposed that these people were genuine hippies. He looked at the tattoo again. "Doesn't that hurt?"

"It's surprising, you get used to it. There's a trick to it; you kind of isolate the pain in your mind. Put a fence around it. There's people who perform operations on themselves, you know—just concentrate incredibly hard and then take some Valium or something and go straight on in. This bloke I read about, right, he studied for months how to do a liver operation: read it all up in the surgery textbooks, got all the gear, sterilized his scalpels, and set to work. Big cut across his belly, tied off all the blood vessels, perfect job. Lifted his stomach aside, reached in—"

"Shut up, Del," said Ollie. "Making me feel sick. And keep still."

"Was there anything wrong with his liver?" said Chris.

"Not when he started," said Derek, and laughed.

Chris was conscious all the time of Jenny: where she was looking, what she was doing. When the kettle boiled and she made the coffee, she said, "Want to come in the garden?" and he got up at once.

The little back garden was tidy, the flower beds weeded and watered, the lawn trimmed. Jenny sat on the step beside the wooden shed, and Chris joined her there, setting his mug down at his feet.

"What happened the other night?" he said. "After I left?"

"I left as well. I climbed out."

"What—without your dress? Or did you go back and put it on? And where were you, anyway? I couldn't see a thing."

"I had a dark shirt and jeans on. That's how I got in in the first place. I wasn't a proper guest, you see. I gate-crashed."

She told him how she'd done it. She had gone into the college as a tourist a couple of days before, with the ball gown concealed in a bag, and had hidden it in the bushes near the boathouse. After dark on the night of the ball she'd climbed the wall that bordered the path outside the college, wearing dark clothes so as not to be seen, and found the bag and changed in the boathouse before joining the rest of the guests.

"You climbed that wall on your own?" said Chris, impressed. "Didn't you go with anyone else?"

"I could hardly go with Derek or Ollie, could I? They'd stand out a bit. Anyway, I like being on me own. I just went to where the music was. Blokes asked me to dance, there was plenty of food and champagne. . .I pretended I'd lost me bloke, you know, when people asked who I was with. Trouble was, I ran into Piers."

She didn't explain how she knew Piers, and Chris didn't ask. But it seemed that Piers had known she'd probably gate-crashed, and he was going to make her pay for it in what she said was the obvious way.

"I hated him," Chris said. "As soon as I heard him and his friends. I hated them all."

"You were brilliant," she said. "I thought they were going to fight you, but you were just fantastic."

He blushed. He didn't know what to say. "Well," he said in the end.

"You don't realize people like that exist anymore," she said. "But they do. Rich and spoiled. . .It's amazing, really; they think they can have everything they want. He's a lord of some sort, Piers. People just *grovel* to him when they know that. If they'd caught me, I wouldn't have had a chance. And no one would have believed me afterward."

Chris wanted to kill Piers and his friends then and there.

"What do you do? Are you a student?" he asked.

"God, no. I'm a parasite. Like them two." She motioned toward Derek and Ollie.

"No, really—"

"I am. I do a bit of waitressing sometimes. That's all. Honest."

"And. . .you live here with. . ."

She was watching him mockingly, knowing what he was trying to ask.

"With Derek and Ollie, yeah," she said.

"Are you. . .I mean. . .is Derek your boyfriend?"

"Why d'you want to know that?"

"Because I was going to ask you to go out with me."

"Go on then."

"Will you go out with me?"

"Yeah. Okay. When?"

"Friday?"

"Fine."

"Have you been to the Jericho Tavern?"

"No. That's the other end of town, isn't it? I only know this end, really."

"They have good bands playing there."

He was dazed by his own good luck. Something must have happened to make him lucky like this, he thought. He drank the coffee, shy again, watching her smooth brown arm and her slender hand as she flicked little stones off the path beside her feet.

"I've got to go," he said. "I've got to be back at work. I'll see you on Friday. I'll call for you here at—"

"No, don't do that. I'll meet you in town. That church thing at the crossroad in the center—what's it called?"

"Carfax."

"That's it. Eight o'clock."

"Right. I'll see you then. Thanks for the coffee."

"Ta-ta, Chris."

It was as easy as that.

For the rest of the week he lived in a daze. When Friday came, he was so jumpy that even his mother, in her own haze of infatuation for Mike Fairfax, felt concerned.

"For God's sake, bring the girl home," she said.

"What girl?"

"The one you're going out with. You wouldn't take that much care if you were just going to see Carl and Jacko. You can't fool your mother."

He hoped that wasn't true. He hadn't told anyone about Jenny, not even Barry Miller, who was the one person he might have been able to tell.

It was a beautiful warm evening when they met, and they didn't go to the Jericho Tavern. Instead they walked to the University Park and sat by the river, just talking.

She told him that she'd left her home in Yorkshire (she didn't tell him why) and that she'd gone first to London, where she knew no one. There she'd drifted into sleeping out, until she met a girl named Tansy, an upper-class dropout with whom she'd become friends. With Tansy she'd come to Oxford, and it had been through Tansy that she'd met Piers.

"It was at a party; I can't remember where. . .one of the colleges. I thought he was nice at first. It was a different world. I'd never seen anything like it; I'd never dreamed people really lived like that. Champagne, so much money— I couldn't believe it. And Piers was a lord, as well. I was tickled pink by that, me going out with a lord. Then I saw what they were *really* like."

Tansy had been supplying Piers with drugs, and Jenny hadn't realized. When Tansy was arrested, Jenny was reduced to sleeping in the night shelter. It was that or Piers's bed.

Finally she had met Derek, and moved in with him and

25

Ollie. They were friends but not lovers, she said; and that was it, really.

Chris knew she wasn't telling him all the truth. She was more complicated than that, and surely she wasn't as naive as she made herself out to be. Still, he didn't challenge her; whatever she said was better than the truth, because she was saying it.

He'd never met a girl remotely like her before. Her face was full of the innocent, alarmed vulnerability he'd seen that night by the lake, and her fragile-seeming bones, her slender arms and hands, made him want to protect her like a baby. He was very conscious of his size, his muscles, his clumsiness beside her.

And at the same time her voice and the way she spoke seemed the opposite of innocent. She sounded sophisticated, but not hard; worldly-wise, but not cynical; mocking, but still kind. She simply seemed much more grown-up than he felt. But for all her awareness of the world, there were huge gaps in her knowledge. It was as if she'd never been to school, as if she'd run wild all her life and never been caught.

"Why don't you go to college?" he said. "You could do some A Levels at the College of Further Education, no problem. Then you could get a place at university."

"Oh, yeah? What would I want to do that for?"

"Because you're intelligent. And if you had a degree, you could get a really good job. And because learning about things is interesting. You could become an M.P. and pass a law to abolish people like Piers."

"Piers isn't the problem. And I can think of a hundred reasons why I wouldn't want to be an M.P. The trouble with people like you is that you think the trouble with people like me is that we're not people like you."

"People like me?"

"People with nice houses and jobs and degrees and stuff. That's not my world, Chris; I'm different. It's not a class thing, if that's what you're thinking."

"I wasn't!"

"It's what you were thinking that I was thinking."

"Eh?"

"Work it out."

He did, and then said, "No, I wasn't. I don't know why it needn't be your world. If you can play language tricks like that, you're more at home in it already than I am. It's anybody's world. And if you're clever, it just seems a waste. . ."

She said nothing, and he felt rebuked; but presently they were talking again, lightly this time, and laughing together. As darkness fell they had to hurry to be out of the park before the gates were locked. They wandered down a narrow lane overhung with dark trees and out into the road called St. Giles', immensely wide, with tall, dignified houses and old stone college buildings on either side.

Under the trees at the foot of the great classical buildings of the Ashmolean Museum, a scruffy little kebab van was parked. Chris bought shish kebabs, and they sat on the museum steps to eat them, disregarding salmonella; love was proof against food poisoning. How she felt about him he couldn't tell, though he thought she probably liked him; but he was in love, intoxicated, drunk with it. Everything about her was perfect, mysterious, miraculous: from the beautiful freesia-like scent she was wearing, to the white ribbon she'd tied around her hair, to the bare brown skin of her delicate feet. His senses were swimming with love; he would have died for her.

As for Jenny. . .she didn't tell him why she'd left home, because she was ashamed. The whole first part of her life was stained with shame and guilt, and yet not a day went past when she didn't return to it, remaking it in her mind, fruitlessly.

She had lived with her parents in the Yorkshire town where she was born. Her father was a warehouseman, her mother a school cook. When Jenny was six years old her father's firm closed down, like so many others in the early eighties, and he could find no other work.

A little while after that, the local council changed the school meal arrangements. Instead of employing their own cooks, the education authority put the service out to tender. Private firms were invited to bid for the contracts. Many women, including Jenny's mother, lost their jobs, and although some of them were taken on by the private caterer, many of them weren't. Jenny's mother was one of the unlucky ones.

So for a long time things were bad in the household. After a year Jenny's mother found another job, as a hospital cleaner this time, but her father was less lucky. He had nothing to do but stay indoors all day, smoking and watching television. Because her mother had to leave the house early in the morning, it was her father who woke Jenny and made her breakfast, and it was then that he began to abuse her.

At first it was just a matter of patting her bare arms, her bare legs, so lightly and casually that it might have meant nothing. But this gradually changed. Patting became stroking, and stroking became squeezing, and by this time Jenny, who was eight, felt hot when it happened and dirty and unhappy afterward.

Then it got worse: foul tobaccoey kisses, hands inside her panties. And worse still. Her mother might have helped, but she was tired and impatient and Jenny couldn't even say it, anyway. She would have liked to tell her teacher, but the school was suffering such a rapid turnover of staff that Jenny knew none of the teachers long enough to trust.

After five years of it, desperate, she got a knife and hid it in her bed. She wasn't sure what she was going to do with it, though she was ready to kill him. When he came to her that morning, she jabbed it at him and cut him on the hand, not badly, but enough to make him bleed a lot. The blood made her feel faint, and it frightened him, too; but when he saw how trivial the wound was, he hit her. From then on the pattern changed. He carried on touching her, but now he hit her as well—cruel, painful blows in places where it didn't show. Jenny had given up expecting help by this time. She'd seen that by taking action herself, she could change things, though not necessarily in ways that she'd wanted. It was a useful lesson.

After another year or so, her father finally got a job. He had to leave the house early, and he had less opportunity to be on his own with his daughter. The abuse slowed down, but that made no difference to Jenny, who'd made her mind up to leave home as soon as she was sixteen. She waited until then because she wanted to be completely, legally free of any obligation to live at home and go to school.

So on the morning of her sixteenth birthday she got up before anyone else in the house, had a last breakfast on her own in the little kitchen, and washed the bowl and the spoon before taking her rucksack and walking out. She left a note saying BYE, MUM, I'LL BE IN TOUCH, and went to the bus station. She caught a coach to the south and left her hometown forever.

Nothing that had happened since had wiped out the shame and the fear and the hatred. She had slept with a number of boys, including Piers; and though some were fun and some were kind and some were attractive, she saw her father looking out of their eyes, and when she closed hers, it was to hide. Maybe, one day, she'd tell someone; maybe she'd tell Chris. But not for a long time yet.

three

On the following Monday, Barry Miller asked Chris to help him with a special job. Chris thought it might have been another ball, but it turned out to be less glamorous than that.

"I got this shed," Barry said, as they drove up through Oxford in the van with Chris's bike in the back. "Well, more of a chalet, really. On the canal. I want to wire it up and decorate it—use it as a workshop or something. Put in a bed, maybe. Make it comfortable."

They went into Kidlington first, two or three miles north of the city, to pick up some bits and pieces from home. Barry lived in a neat little house in a modern development. They got there at about four o'clock, and Barry's wife, Sue, offered to make them a cup of tea.

She worked as a school secretary, she told Chris. Their ten-year-old son, Sean, was playing soccer outside, and Barry stopped and kicked the ball about before taking a shot

31

that banged against the garage door, where the goal was. Sue rolled her eyes. She was a pretty woman, blond and quiet, with an odd air of cheerful common sense shadowed by anxiety, as if someone near to her—her son, perhaps—was better now, but had recently had a serious illness from which he wasn't quite free. Chris found himself warming to her at once. It was curious that in the van on the way there Barry had asked him not to mention the shed to Sue; but she seemed to understand her husband and didn't ask what job they were on.

"How long have you lived in Oxford, Chris?" she said, as Barry showed Sean how to bend the ball around a defender.

"All my life. I was born here. D'you come from London?"

"Yeah. We moved here three years ago. We were going to go to Australia, but my parents are getting on, you know how it is. . . . Barry's happy, anyway. Have you left school? You look too old. . ."

"I've got another year. Then I do my A Levels and try for university. Sue, d'you think if a person's clever enough, they should go to university and use their talent?"

"If they've got the chance, yes," she said. "I'm doing a degree now with the Open University. It's amazing. It's the most exciting thing I've ever done. I'm learning so much. . . . I'm doing English literature. Barry thinks I must be really clever, but I keep telling him he's cleverer than me; he should do a course too. But he's practical, clever with his hands, really."

"He's busy," said Chris. "The firm's got a lot of work on."

"Yes," she said, nodding, looking out at the neat lawn, their happy son. "It's come on well. It was probably the right thing to do, to come here."

Barry and Sue were fond of each other in a way Chris admired enormously. They seemed to like each other, to tease and tolerate and laugh with each other, as well as being close physically. When Barry had come in, he had embraced her, and she had hugged him back tightly. And he obviously loved his son and was loved in return. There was one moment that Chris saw through the window as he drank his tea: Barry was dribbling the ball, and Sean tackled him and surprised them both by winning it. Barry turned deftly and got the ball back from Sean's feet, then spun and shot in the same movement. It was an excellent shot. The ball hit the garage with a deafening *clang*. But in the shooting, Barry lost his balance and sat down with a sudden thump on his backside. It was Sean's reaction that captivated Chris: his laughing, flushed expression showed him simultaneously admiring his father's shot, laughing at the comic fall, and becoming concerned in case he'd hurt himself. Somehow in that expression Chris saw a lifetime of love, an image of what a family should be. A look like that on your son's face would be something to be proud of.

On their way to the shed by the canal, Barry told Chris about Sean.

"He's the king of the world as far as I'm concerned," he said. "He takes after his mum in all the good ways. He's quick and clever, but he's kindhearted, too, you know what I mean? He's not soft—I don't mean that. I mean he's kind...he's a kind boy. I worry about him sometimes."

"Why? He seems really happy."

"You never know what can happen. I used to know some villains... I've seen some bad things. I've done some bad things, come to that. Once you look under the surface, kind of thing, you never feel safe, not really."

Chris didn't know what he meant. They turned off the highway and down past the motel, toward the village of Wolvercote. They went over the steep canal bridge and almost immediately took a right turn along a rough track under the trees.

"I haven't been along here for years," Chris said. "I'd forgotten all about it."

"Good," said Barry. "The less people know about this place, the better."

"Why? You going to open a secret casino or something?"

Barry said nothing until they pulled up, about a half-mile along the canal, in a clearing beside a cluster of tumbledown farm buildings.

"No," he said finally. "Just a place to go to ground in. Keep out of sight for a while."

"What for?" said Chris, getting out with him. "Is someone after you? I mean, you know, don't tell me if you don't
want to, but. . ."

Barry looked around. In his yellow polo shirt and light
trousers, he looked young, tough, cool—like an actor playing the hero in a thriller.

"Listen, Chris," he said. "I'm going to trust you, okay.
You're a bright kind of bloke. I can't tell Dave or Tony;
they haven't got two brains to rub together. But I gotta tell
someone. The thing is, a few years back I had a run-in with
this family, right. Three brothers—name of Carson. They
were villains; they were evil. Actually they were worse
than villains. They had connections with terrorism. Irish,
you know, paramilitaries. . . . They stuck together like the
Mafia. Code of honor. Anyway, I had something to do with
putting two of 'em behind bars. . . . Straight up, honest. So I
gotta be careful. They won't touch Sue or Sean; that'd be
well out of order. But, you know, just in case. That's why I
got this place. You never said anything to her?"

"Not a word."

"Good lad. She'd only worry. So it's just a matter of
wiring it up, really. Make it habitable. Nothing posh; couple
of lights, sockets, storage heaters. Day's work, maybe. Like
I said, Dave or Tony'd be talking all over the place, all
mouth. . . . Good lads, mind you, fair old workers. . . .
Grab hold of this."

He handed Chris a roll of heavy cable from the back of
the van and took a tool box and various fittings himself,

then led the way to a substantial-looking shed half-buried in nettles. It was made of precast concrete panels, and the roof was of corrugated iron, and despite the air of decay all around, it was impressively solid. Barry turned a key, and they walked in. The concrete floor was unbroken; there was no smell of dampness. There was even a working electric light, with a fluorescent tube mounted clumsily on the wooden beams holding up the roof.

"Not bad, eh? Well built, you can say that for it. I'm going to insulate it, put some fiberglass stuff in the roof, panel the walls, do it all decent. There's water laid on, look. . ." He jerked his head at a metal sink in a corner. "Could put a shower in, actually, now I think of it. You done any plumbing? Shouldn't be too hard to put a toilet in, really, should it? Common sense, really. Yeah, little shower room, toilet, kitchenette. . . be worth a bit, wouldn't it, eh? There's an idea in that, you know. Holiday chalets. Get the design right, and bingo. Property in Europe, now, that's dirt cheap. Get in quick. That's a good idea, that . . ."

What Chris liked about Barry was his quickness. A minute before he'd been full of dark hints about Mafia-style revenge, and now here he was making a mental fortune by building holiday chalets in Europe.

However much wishful thinking went into his forward planning, he was practical enough when it came to details. He'd made a wiring design that Chris had no difficulty in understanding, and all the cable, the fittings, and the tools were soon out of the van and in a neat pile on the concrete floor.

"Course, strictly speaking I shouldn't take this out of the business, being as it's a private dwelling. It's going down as a business expense, though, taxwise. I always pay me taxes. Some blokes don't, but it's a mug's game. It might take 'em years, but they get you in the end. Right, Chris. You all right to cope with this?"

Chris nodded. "There's one thing on this plan. . . . You don't want a switch by the door? A main switch for the lights?"

"Ah, I knew I'd forgotten something. I'm going to get one of them infrared detectors, right, so as soon as anyone comes near the shed, the lights come on. It's going to go there, outside the door, with a timer on it. So as soon as you come near the shed, the lights go on automatically, and you got a minute to open the door and go to the switch inside by the electricity meter. After a minute the timer switch cuts out, but by that time you got the other switch on, see, to override it and leave the lights on."

"Is a minute enough? Suppose you drop the keys or something?"

"You can set it to any time you want—ten seconds, ten minutes. . ."

It looked a bit overcomplicated to Chris. If the infrared unit failed, you'd have to fumble about near the floor in the dark before you found the light switch. However, it was easy enough to understand.

"Where's the infrared detector?" he said, looking at the pile on the floor.

"It's a special one. I had to order it. It ain't come in yet. Just treat it like a normal switch; put the wire there, like it says in the diagram, and tape it up safely. We'll put the infrared switch in when it gets here. Okay? Can you get on with it on your own, then, now you know where it is? Take the key, look; I'll give you the key—I've got a spare. I reckon it'll take a day. That fair?"

"I reckon so," said Chris, thinking he could do it in half that time. "Easily."

"So I'll unload your bike now and leave you to it. Start tomorrow, start now—do it when you like. I'll expect you. . .what's today? Monday? I'll expect you in on Wednesday morning, with the job done. Give us a call if you hit a problem."

Chris pocketed the key and watched the van bump away down the shady track under the trees. Soon there was no sound at all but birdsong and the perpetual distant drone of traffic on the highway, but that was so muffled by the leaves that it was hardly there at all. The little group of huts lay drenched, drowned in green; ivy was swarming over walls, nettles were crowding at the doors, tall rank grass had obliterated pathways. Chris spent a few minutes looking around the other buildings (a chicken house, what looked like a milking shed, and something else that had nearly fallen down) before looking for the canal. It was invisible, though he knew it must be less than a stone's throw away; the encircling green—a burgeoning riot of leaves, twigs, branches, grass, weeds—disoriented him.

Finally he saw a gap in the bushes and pushed through it to come out onto the empty towpath.

The canal was quiet, narrow, and brown. A blue dragonfly skimmed the surface. Some way off to the right a small abandoned cabin cruiser lay half-sunk, gently sliding into decay, some of its molecules no doubt already blooming triumphantly in the reeds that grew alongside. Chris had watched the canal from the bridge in Wolvercote. Half a dozen narrow boats a day, if that, passed along, with vacationers sunning themselves as they manipulated the lock gates or leaned on the tiller. There was no one in sight now, no other creature but the dragonfly and an incurious brown horse in the parched meadow across the canal.

Chris went back through the bushes to the shed—or chalet. He could see it vividly as Barry saw it: cedar-clad, with plate glass windows, a patio with a table under an umbrella, window boxes cascading brightly colored flowers, Barry and Sue and Sean, perhaps in swimsuits around a barbecue. It was an illustration from a holiday brochure.

The reality was less glamorous. The interior of the shed was just a blank space. It could have served equally well as an artist's studio, a temporary classroom in a crowded school, or a Central American torture chamber. Alone, happy, apprehensive, Chris began to sort out the tools and the cable for the job, and, as always when he was alone, he let himself daydream. Soon it was not Barry who lived there but himself and Jenny. Her slender ironical presence already filled the clearing like a ghost.

Barry's story of the Carson brothers was partly true. It had nothing to do with terrorism, though. Nor had Barry's name always been Miller.

He'd been living in South London. His name was Barry Springer, and he was working as an electrician. He'd become involved in a casual way with two brothers named Frank and Billy Carson, who liked to think of themselves as gang leaders, like the famous Kray twins. And, like the Krays' world, that of the Carsons overlapped the fringes of show business. Barry enjoyed the feeling of danger and glamour; he especially liked mixing with half-famous people like snooker players and TV actors, buying them drinks in clubs, being regarded by them as one of the Carson gang.

In fact, the Carson brothers were incompetent thugs. They'd carried out a number of robberies from jewelers' shops without being caught, but without getting rich, either. They decided to rob a Securicor van delivering money to a bank, and with the money from that to buy their way into a big drugs operation.

But Barry Springer had a conscience about drugs. He had a slight conscience about theft anyway, but at least money was clean. He decided privately that the Securicor job would be his last, and that he'd take his share of the money and go somewhere else to start up a little business.

The robbery went wrong. The Carson brothers were carrying guns, which they'd never done before, and the Securicor guards were far more alert than they'd expected. Billy Carson panicked and shot one of them; the guard died at once, and the gang fled with only a fraction of the money they'd hoped for.

Over the next couple of days the Carsons ran wild, as if they knew they were finished. They shot and wounded a building society cashier and got away with four thousand pounds; they shot and killed a sub-postmaster and stole three hundred; and then by pure chance they got their biggest haul of all. They were driving about more or less at random when they saw another security van, this time taking money away from a bank.

If they hadn't been drinking, and desperate, and if they hadn't known they were doomed, they'd never have tried it. But on the spur of the moment Frank Carson pulled the car to the curb, and ninety seconds later they were speeding away through the South London streets with a hundred and forty-seven thousand pounds in the car and two men lying dead on the pavement behind them.

They hid the car and the money at once in a garage they rented behind a row of shops in Deptford. While Billy went home to pack, Frank went to a travel agent's to buy tickets for Spain. He never got home. When he got off the bus, he could sense that something was wrong; and as he turned the corner and saw the police marksmen outside the block of council flats, the roadblock, the megaphones, he knew that Billy was either going to be taken prisoner or shot.

He quickly stepped back into the main street and took a bus to the garage. At least with the money he could lie low and get another passport, his own still being in the flat with Billy.

41

But the money was gone. Frank knew that the only other person who knew about the garage was Barry Springer, who hadn't been on any jobs since the first Securicor one when Billy had shot the guard.

Frank was a little cooler-headed than Billy, but not much—not enough to prevent himself from getting in the car and speeding to Barry Springer's house in a fury.

It was too late. Springer wasn't there, nor were his wife and his small son. Instead, Frank burst through the door to find himself facing armed policemen lying in wait for him. He was arrested at once.

By that time Billy had been shot dead. He had wounded two policemen in the gunfight; one of them died in the hospital. Frank was tried for murder and sentenced to life imprisonment. The chief witness for the prosecution was Barry Springer. Because he'd turned Queen's evidence, he was not charged himself. He was allowed to go free. He changed his name to Miller and moved away from London with his family; the police helped him to cover his tracks.

But Frank and Billy Carson had a younger brother. His name was Edward, and he was quite a different character. Where they were impulsive, he was calculating; where they were stupid, he was intelligent. He'd taken no part in their criminal activities, not because of any moral scruples, but because he thought crime was an inefficient way to get what you could also get, and more importantly keep, by means of cunning. He had trained as a chartered accountant, and with that cover he had developed ways of making stolen money look clean. He was already wealthy.

He might have been contemptuous of his elder brothers' shortsighted brutality, except for one thing: they had jointly and tenderly brought him up after the death of their elderly parents, and he loved both of them with the only love in his life.

Edward was a strange, cruel, philosophical man; a great reader; a man whose passions were as chilly and implacable as a glacier. So when Billy was killed and Frank sent to prison for what would be at least twenty-five years, that icy intelligence turned toward Barry Springer. Springer had betrayed Billy; Springer had stood in the witness box swearing with wide-eyed innocence that he had no idea where the money was. And that had meant an even heavier sentence for Frank, since the jury simply didn't believe him when he said Springer must have taken it.

The one passion that can take root in the frozen soil of a nature like Edward Carson's is revenge. Springer was responsible; Springer would pay. Carson had found an outlet for his talent and a use for his wealth. He began to look for Barry Springer.

four

From start to finish on Tuesday, the job took Chris five hours. By the end of it all the old wiring was replaced with new, and there was a ring main circuit with four double sockets on it, a radial circuit for a cooker, and a lighting circuit with two ceiling roses. In addition, Chris had thought of a variation on Barry's infrared idea, and put in the wiring for it: a floodlight mounted on the outside of the shed, which could also be switched on or off from inside.

When he'd finished, he checked that everything worked, that all the cable was securely tucked alongside the wooden battens that were going to carry plasterboard, and that all the sawdust and odd bits of cable and flexible cord and plastic were swept up. It was three in the afternoon, and he'd finished for the day.

He locked the shed and pushed his bike along the track. It was too rough for a good road bike; you could slam about on it with a mountain bike, but to Chris mountain bikes were clumsy, heavy things. No one needed a mountain bike in Oxford, so almost by definition anyone who rode one was a poser. Chris's idea of cycling was the speed and courage of the Tour de France; he saved his wheels for the road.

When he came out at Wolvercote, he got on at once and rode hard, head down, for the Cowley Road. It took him fifteen minutes to get to Jenny's house, where he found no one in. He hadn't actually arranged to meet her, but he still felt disappointed.

He cruised up and down for a few minutes before swinging away from the Cowley Road and heading for Rose Hill.

This was an area of small roads and semidetached houses at the south of the city, where his father had been living for the past six months with Diane, his mistress. Chris wasn't sure why he was going there now, except that he didn't want to go home.

He was surprised to see a FOR SALE sign outside the house, but when Diane answered the door, he forgot it at once. She was pretty, blond, plumpish, about twenty-three or twenty-four years old. Chris had known her since she'd come to work in his father's office two years before.

"Chris! Hi. Er, come in. Your dad's in the garden."

He wished he didn't blush so easily. It was Diane's being so pretty, and it was her short skirt and bare legs, and the warm flowery afternoon air, and it was the way she was smiling at him, too, as if she liked him.

He went through the narrow living room and out through the French window into the sunny little back garden.

"Hi, Dad," he said.

His father, in shorts and a T-shirt and a Panama hat for his balding head, looked up from the papers on the board across his lap.

"Hello, boy," he said. "What the hell do you want, then?"

This was a standard greeting. His father was very fond of him, and Chris knew it.

"How's it going?"

"Business is booming, son. That's why I'm sitting here doing it in the sunshine. How's Mum?"

"Fine. Mike Fairfax is living with. . ."

He was going to say *us,* but that wouldn't have been true. Mike Fairfax was sleeping with Chris's mother, not living with him. His father brightened with interest.

"Really? Fairfax the philosopher?"

"Yes. She's gone all political. She wears badges and goes to meetings and things."

He sat on the step of the patio and held out his hand to the black-and-white kitten playing there. The little creature batted suspiciously at it before running away to hide under a lavender bush.

"I know the type," his father said. "Fairfax, I mean. Don't tell me, he's Labour, isn't he? Can't be a Liberal. Must be Labour. Am I right?"

"Even if I said no, you'd tell me I was making a mistake."

"Stands out a mile. He's got a social conscience, I can tell. I never had one of them. Your mum was shocked when she found out. I remember, soon after we got married, the big thing then was saving the tiger. I said save the bloody tiger, good idea; we can use it for medical experiments, get a lot more experiments per tiger than per rat. She didn't take to that. Serious woman, you see. Still, if old Fairfax is keeping her warm, fair enough. Thank you, Diane, bless you."

Diane had appeared with a tray of tea and a plate of greasy-looking homemade biscuits. His father reached down and took one.

"You're getting fat," Chris said.

"Fat? What's that? Would you say I was fat, Diane?"

"Yeah," she said. "You're a shapeless old lump."

She tipped his hat over his face and went inside.

"You see how she treats me?" said his father, delighted, his mouth full of biscuit.

"Did Diane make these?" Chris asked him.

"Yes. Don't you like 'em?"

"They're very nice, yeah. Are you working from home now, Dad?"

"When I can. No point in going into the office if I can sit here and do it. Not a lot of work about now, anyway. I'm doing an extension for some rich geezer out at Charlbury at the moment. I talked him into having his whole house redone. He's made a lot of money, so he wants it classical; that's what all the yuppies like—pediments and columns and that. I can fake it easy enough, but I hate it, really. I thought I'd do a kind of Florentine dome on his garage, except he'd probably spot I was pulling his leg."

"You shouldn't do it if you hate it. That's just prostitution."

"Pays the rent. Nothing immoral about paying the rent."

"Yeah, but. . .you should do what your talent tells you, not what some rich bloke decides."

"I am. My talent's for faking. Anyway, he's paying; he can have what he wants. I make sure it won't fall down and the rain won't come in."

He frowned, fumbled in his trouser pocket, and pulled out a tattered tube of indigestion tablets.

"Flaming biscuits," he said, thickly chewing a tablet. "Always give me heartburn. She's a wonderful girl, you know, Diane. Tremendous talent."

"Talent?"

"For architecture."

"Really?"

He hoped he didn't sound skeptical. He didn't mean to.

"Yeah," his father went on. "She's wasted as a secretary. She's going to do the Polytechnic course. What about you? What are you doing with yourself?"

Chris told him about Barry Miller and the job. He wondered if he should mention the hideaway, and thought it wouldn't matter as long as he didn't say where it was.

"Gangsters after him?" his father said. "He's having you on. What he wants is a love nest."

"He's not like that!"

"Betcher. Somewhere to take a girlfriend. That's why he didn't want you to tell his wife. We don't have gangsters running around, not in Oxford."

"He's not like that," Chris said stubbornly. The idea of Barry deceiving Sue and Sean, breaking up that close and loving family, was horrible.

"Oh, well, I suppose I can talk," said his father, sighing. "Oh, I know what I was going to ask you. We're going away, me and Diane, just for the weekend. Friday to Sunday. You couldn't pop in and keep an eye on the cat, could you?"

"Yeah. Sure."

"Little bastard shits everywhere, eats everything, and bites. It'd suit me if you could get him run over, but Diane'd be upset, so you'd better not. Just feed him and water him. I'd ask the neighbors, but we had words the other day; they're a dodgy bunch. We're not going to stay here long."

"Oh, yeah! I saw the FOR SALE sign outside. Where are you going?"

"Out Long Hanborough way. We've got a place already. Filthy dirty old cottage; the outside toilet's the only thing holding it up. I got Mike Lovell working on it now. He did the kitchen extension, remember him? As soon as it's ready we'll move out there so this'll be vacant for a buyer. Here, you could stay here over the weekend, if you wanted. Give

49

Mum and Fairfax a run of the house on their own. Have some mates in here, if you'd like. Have a party and annoy the neighbors."

"Yeah! Right, I will."

Chris knew instantly what he was going to do that weekend. He said good-bye to his father, having arranged to pick up the key on Friday afternoon, and went back through the French window. He looked around for Diane, to say good-bye, and found her coming downstairs. She looked past him and shut the living room door so that they were alone in the hall together.

"Chris," she said quietly. "Your mum...is she all right?"

"*He* kept asking that," Chris told her. "Yes, she's fine, honest."

"Because she's such a nice person. I'd hate it if she was, you know, unhappy or anything. I couldn't bear that."

"Well, she was at first. But I think she's okay now. She's actually got this boyfriend, so probably she's not going to commit suicide or anything."

She gave him a complicated look and twisted her mouth. She looked even younger than Jenny. She was so close that he could smell the soap she'd been using.

"I couldn't bear it if everyone thought, you know, I was just..."

"Course they don't," said Chris vaguely. "Dad says you're going to do an architecture course at the Poly."

"Yeah. It was his idea, really. It looks interesting."

They stood awkwardly for a second or so, two people

closer in age, personality, and manner to each other than either was to the man outside, the father, the lover. Then Diane gave a rueful little smile and opened the door for him to leave.

five

Chris's mother was quite happy for him to stay at his father's house over the weekend. He hadn't known what her reaction would be; she'd become unpredictable since taking up with Mike Fairfax, or else Chris had become less good at guessing. He'd been afraid that she'd make a scene, treat it as desertion, taking his father's side against her, and so on. In fact, she seemed pleased.

"How is he?" she said that evening as the three of them sat at supper.

"He kept asking how *you* were. He's fine. He's getting fat."

"Good," she said.

"Good?"

"Well, if he's not worried about getting fat, he won't do what that man in Switzerland did."

"Man in Switzerland?" said Mike Fairfax.

"The year before last," Chris told him, "when we were on holiday, there was this middle-aged bloke in the hotel with a really young girl. She was half his age, and he was obviously trying to impress her with how fit he was. Everywhere we went we'd see him jogging or swimming or doing push-ups, and she was trailing along behind looking dead bored. They have these exercise runs marked out in the forest, with wooden apparatus set up, so you run a bit, then do bench jumps and chin-ups, and then run a bit more. Anyway, he was out one morning impressing her and he had a heart attack and snuffed it, just like that."

Mike made a noncommittal reply and helped himself to some grapes. He went running every morning himself, which was why Chris had told the story. He was a good man, Chris could see that; he was concerned and committed and energetic and kind and decent. He was particularly keen to involve Chris in things, to defer to him politely as an inhabitant of the house of longer standing, to treat him as a sensible, intelligent adult. It was one of the biggest mysteries in the world, Chris thought, how someone who did all the right things could be so irritating.

However, Mike wasn't important. The only important thing was Jenny, and the fact that Chris was going to see her the following evening.

Some of Barry Miller's lighting equipment was on hire to a theater group that was performing *Romeo and Juliet* in one of the college gardens. Chris had asked Jenny to go to it with him, and she had agreed. Chris had bought the tickets

53

and washed and shaved and dressed in his sharpest casual clothes, and by the time he was standing outside the college lodge, where they'd agreed to meet, he was shaking with nerves.

He had no idea why, except that this was a formal kind of date, something he'd never done before. But when she turned the corner into the narrow medieval street, looking so fresh and sweet and wise, his heart nearly burst with pride and love, and he found his hands reaching out for her of their own accord, almost. Hers responded. They stood for a silly second or two smiling at each other, and he thought, This is the first time we've touched.

The stage was a wooden floor under the trees, with the seats built up in tiers around it. They sat high up and watched the story unfold, a little patch of tragic light in the gathering darkness. Chris hardly noticed it. All his attention was focused on Jenny, on her hand in his, on the delicate curve of her bare neck, on the fresh freesia-like smell of her perfume, the same one he'd smelled on the ball gown in the boathouse.

During the intermission she said, "I've never seen a Shakespeare play before. We did this at school, but I never paid any attention. It was all mixed up with *West Side Story*, and we had to do our own modern version with punks and that. I didn't know it'd be like this."

"Don't you like it?"

"It's wonderful!"

At the end she cried. At least, she wiped her eyes with

the back of her hand and sniffed. Chris found himself more moved by that than by the play itself.

They walked out through the lamplit garden, holding hands, and a tense expectation seemed to be hanging in the air, like heavy fruit on the trees all around.

Outside the garden, in the narrow cobbled lane with the high garden wall on one side and the ancient stone of a college on the other, she said, "I was wondering. . ."

"Yes?"

"I was wondering if you were ever going to get around to kissing me."

He let his bicycle fall and put his arms around her. He'd expected warmth and softness, but never in this degree, and never combined with a lithe and sinuous strength that seemed to quiver like a flame in his arms.

Dazed with it, he hardly knew how much time had passed when they drew apart. They were standing a little way from an old streetlight mounted on the college wall, and her half-shadowed face looked strong and mysterious, like an Aztec sculpture.

"I don't understand you," she said.

"Why? What d'you mean?"

"I mean you obviously want to, but you hang back. There's nothing to be afraid of."

"No. It's difficult to explain. I think it's—"

"Don't *explain*. You don't have to *explain*."

"But you said you didn't understand, so I was—"

"I don't want to understand, necessarily. I think you're

strange, but I don't mind your being strange; it's nothing I want altered or anything. I like you as you are."

"Do you?"

"I just said so."

"I love you, Jenny."

He'd said it. He hadn't meant to, but there it was.

Suddenly, with a little convulsion that felt like a sob, she was kissing him again. Her lips were open and moist, it was honeydew, he was drinking the essence of her and it was making him drunk with wonder.

"Listen," he whispered when they finally stopped kissing. "My father's got a house in Rose Hill, okay, and he's going away for the weekend and he's asked me to stay there and look after his cat."

"Yeah, and. . ."

"Would you come and stay with me?"

"When?"

"Friday night. And Saturday."

"Okay."

He searched his memory exhaustively later on in bed, after he'd walked her home and they'd shared a pizza and one beer, which was all they could afford, in the kitchen of the squat with a girl named Marje. Jenny wouldn't let him come to her bedroom, but she'd promised to come to his father's house; he was sure she had. He replayed their kisses and her words over and over again. He was sure he'd got it right.

When Friday came, and he was sitting in the narrow living room at Rose Hill, his certainty began to fade. The kitten for whose sake he was there was curled up asleep on the sofa, and the setting sun threw a warm glow over the Victorian tiled fireplace, the shelves of books beside it, his father's neatly stacked architectural journals and art books, the shabby but beautiful Persian rug. Chris sat in the silence, feeling the house empty all around him, prepared for her. There was food in the kitchen: a cold quiche and salad, laid out by Diane. There was music; his father was not one to live without his cassettes and his compact discs: Wagner, Mahler, Bruckner, Strauss.

The whole house was theirs. . . . Chris began to tremble. He'd got it wrong. She hadn't said she'd come. She wasn't going to come; she had no intention of coming. She'd laughed when he'd said he loved her, and he'd blanked it out of his memory. He'd never had pizza and beer in the kitchen of the squat; he'd dreamed the whole thing. She was sitting with Derek and Ollie now, laughing at him. He imagined every kind of humiliation as he sat there in the neat little room while the evening faded and the night began to gather in the garden.

When it was completely dark he stood up slowly, feeling the tension in his muscles. The kitten looked up briefly and meowed before instantly falling asleep again. Chris reached for the light switch, and as the lamp came on, his reflection sprang into being in the French window, looking imprisoned and desolate.

In case she'd mistaken the number of the house and was wandering up and down looking for the most likely one, he went out the front door and stood in the tiny garden. There was no one in sight. Identical little brick houses stretched to the right and the left on both sides of the road. Lights were on behind curtained windows, streetlights gleamed off the roofs of parked cars or lit up the pale green underside of the tall trees on the pavement, shining on no one.

He could hear traffic from the main road around the corner, and music from someone's open window across the road, and laughter from a back garden. Along with the heavy fragrance of night-scented stocks from next door, there was a trace of charcoal smoke in the air, and the smell of grilling meat.

He walked slowly out into the center of the road, down to the end, and turned, then went all the way back past the house to the other end. Not one car turned into the street, not one star fell out of the sky, not one girl appeared around the corner.

Chris felt a physical pain in his chest. He was ready to cry out with his longing for her. He knew exactly, almost to the yard, how far her house was from this. He felt an invisible cord joining the two of them, stretching tightly through the night from his heart to hers. He imagined her house now: a bedroom light upstairs, her room, which she'd forbidden him to see; her room, full of her scent, with her clothes tossed over the back of a chair, her shoes, the little radio that whispered to her in the night, the little mirror that gazed at her, the bedside light that shone on her silky olive skin. . .

He was seized with the desire to go there right then. He could visualize every step of the way. He'd just stand outside, see that her light was on, and know where she was; that would be enough—he'd be happy with that.

And simultaneously he thought how foolish he was. He wouldn't know which of the windows in the little house was hers. He might be gazing lovestruck at Derek's or Ollie's. Or else, on the way there, he might miss her as she came to Rose Hill by a different route. Then she'd arrive here and find the house empty, and leave again. No! He'd have to keep faith and wait.

He wandered slowly back, tracing the letters of her name on every paving stone, on every gatepost, making the whole road hers.

A last look around, and he went inside again. On the table in the kitchen he'd put two plates, two knives and forks, two glasses. How pathetic it all looked. He picked up her plate, then realized that he wasn't hungry anyway, and put everything away.

In the living room, still and silent in the lamplight, the kitten was waking up and looking for something to play with. Chris picked it up. It was so small and light that it was hardly there at all, but it was full of life and energy, batting at his hand with a pawful of soft needles, leaping sideways out of his grasp and running away, only to stalk back again, rolling over and spitting at imaginary threats.

"You don't need anyone, do you, Thing?" he said to it. "You've got everything you want. You've got everyone organized. . . . They bring you food and play with you and clear up after you, and you don't know anything about it, do you? And you don't care, either. You lucky little bastard. If I told you about Jenny, you wouldn't even laugh. You wouldn't know what I was talking about. Just because I saw her at that ball in her long dress under the trees. . . . I'm lost, I don't know what to do. . ."

The kitten took no notice. Quite suddenly, after plucking savagely at the Persian rug, which had had the effrontery to snag its little claws, the kitten lay down and fell asleep at once. Chris touched it gently and went to bed.

six

He woke early in the strange bed and lay for a while in the warm yellow light coming through the curtains, pretending that he'd lost his memory and didn't know who he was. It was no good, though; he couldn't forget her for long enough, or ignore how humiliated he felt.

At eight o'clock he got up, heavy-hearted, and put on shorts and a T-shirt before going down to give Thing its milk and make some breakfast for himself. He took a bowl of cornflakes into the garden, which was already hot, and sat on the bottom step to eat them.

He'd just gone in to put the kettle on when the doorbell rang. Instantly his heart started thudding, but it was only the postman with a parcel that was too big to go in the mailbox. Chris went back to the kitchen and made some tea, wondering what to do for the rest of the day; and then the doorbell rang for the second time.

This time it was Jenny.

She stood on the step, half-shy, half-defiant, and said, "I couldn't come last night after all. I'd've rung, but. . . "

"I've just made some tea," he said.

He stood aside. As she passed him in the doorway she hesitated and then leaned up and kissed him clumsily before going through, and there it was—his heart had melted again.

They were both shy with each other. He poured the tea for them, and they sat on the step watching Thing chase a butterfly.

"I thought you weren't going to come," he said.

"I said I would. You should believe people when they tell you things."

"I do. I believe everything."

She sipped her tea, holding the mug in both hands. The clear sunlight showed up a bloom on her skin that was like that on a plum: the faintest powdery clouding imaginable over the delicate rose-olive underneath. She seemed to enjoy his gaze; she turned and smiled.

"*Who's* this place belong to?" she said.

"My dad. He lives here with his girlfriend. They've gone to Paris for the weekend."

"What's he do, your dad?"

"He's an architect. She—his girlfriend, Diane—she's his secretary. Or used to be. He reckons she's talented at architecture, so she's going to the Poly to do a course."

"Perhaps she is."

"Well...yeah, perhaps she is."

"Was there a big fight? When they split up, him and your mum? Was it painful?"

"There wasn't a scene, no. It was all very civilized, I suppose. You know, kind of *we're too mature to behave in a vulgar kind of way and throw things, goodness, let's be sophisticated.* . . . Actually, Mum was devastated, I think. She used to stay in her bedroom all day and get drunk. I did all the shopping and cooking and stuff. Then one day she met this bloke—he's living with us now—and she was all right again. She went back to treating me like a kid, even though I'd been looking after her all that time."

"It doesn't sound as if you like her very much."

"Like her? Oh, no, she's fine, she's all right. I can't stand him, though."

"Your dad?"

"No! Her bloke. He's all creepy and wimpy, you know. He wants everyone to like him, so he tries too hard. Dad's not a bit like that. He couldn't give a shit. He pretends not to, anyway, but I know he cares about art and architecture and music and things like that. You wouldn't think so to look at him. He's fat and bald and he looks all scruffy and lazy, but he really does know a hell of a lot, and he really cares, too. Not about making an impression, but about truth and honesty and doing things well."

"Do you love him?"

"Yeah, I do. Yeah."

"What about his girlfriend?"

"Diane? Oh, she's really young; she's blond and pretty and. . . oh, well, I suppose she might be really talented at architecture, but that's not the first thing you'd think about. You know, you see her and Dad together and somehow you don't think they spend much time discussing architecture."

"Have you got any brothers or sisters?"

"No. You?"

"No. Thank God." Then she put her mug down on the step and looked up at him and said, "Come indoors."

He stood up, his heart beating fast, and followed her in through the French window to the little living room. She half turned. He caught her wrist, bare flesh under his fingers, and then they were in each other's arms, kissing so fiercely that it bruised their lips.

After a minute they drew back, breathless, and each of them saw an urgent brightness in the other's eyes. With no word said, they took hands and made for the stairs.

In his room they sat on the unmade bed. He said, "Get up a sec," and threw off the covers altogether, so that the bed was bare, a clear white surface. They lay down together. She was so slender and light that she hardly made any impression on the bed. He could smell her hair—sweet, as if she'd just washed it. She looked up at him briefly, and then her eyes moved away and she wriggled down so that her head was on the pillow beside his elbow. The movement made her short flowered skirt ride up over her thighs. She made no move to push it down.

He leaned down to kiss her. She moved her head a little to make it easier, and they found each other's mouths touching—brushing at first gently back and forth, up and down, with the outside of their lips, holding themselves back. Then as he moved his mouth down toward her chin she let her lower lip go with it, and he found himself kissing the slick silky moistness inside, and he touched it with his tongue like a delicate small fish.

He found his tongue being touched by hers in return, his lips nibbled with the utmost tenderness; and then they were eating, drinking, licking, swallowing, exploring the inside of each other's mouths with perfect freedom.

His hand was still on her arm. He moved it gently and brushed her breast: the softest thing in the world, a cloud, a thought. And there was her nipple under his palm, through the cotton T-shirt, innocent somehow in its little firmness, and he stroked it with his fingertips. It was like a small animal nosing at him, curious and self-possessed, and he found himself smiling with delight.

Her hands were moving on him too: his ribs, his thigh, his bare stomach. Again they kissed, and again, more strongly now. He pressed the length of his body against her and felt, happily, a equal pressure answering him.

Then she pulled free and sat up. With one swift movement she pulled the T-shirt over her head, and then stood up to slip off her skirt and panties. He gasped in wonder at the little dove breasts, pink-tipped, the softest delicate curve of

65

silky belly, the pearl luster sheen of thigh and buttock, and the neat frank patch of black hair. It—she—her body—her expression, flushed, excited, confiding—was as lovely as the night of the ball had been. . .that extraordinary moment when she'd appeared out of the darkness beside the lake, needing his help.

Every scrap of shyness and doubt had vanished, and in a few seconds he was naked as well. Instantly they were pressed together, hugging each other close, their bare legs tangling, hands pressing each other's backs.

She broke away and sat up, breathing quickly.

"Wait," she said, and reached down to the canvas bag she'd dropped beside the bed.

"I've got—" he said.

"It's all right."

She came up clutching something in a closed fist. He knelt up to face her and saw something that had been concealed before: a small, perfect butterfly tattooed at the top of her left buttock.

"You didn't. . .not Ollie—"

"God, no!" she said, gasping. "I wouldn't let him near me, don't worry. This is a *professional* butterfly."

"I love it," he said.

They came together again. Now that they were upright, both his hands were free to run down her flanks, over the slight slim swell of her hips, and cup her soft buttocks. Again and again he kissed her cheeks, her neck, her shoulders; and she took his head and pressed it to her breasts, those dove-soft gentle urgent generous roundnesses, and he kissed and kissed them, drunk with love, until she fell on the bed again and they lay together.

"Just a second," she whispered, twisting around. She opened her hand and tore open the little packet she was holding. It was a condom.

He said, "I bought some—"

"It's all right, shh. . . ."

She knelt up and, teasingly slow, gently put it on him. For a vanishing second he felt sorrowful: she'd done this before; she wasn't altogether new to it as he was. Then she lay down again, and he began to stroke her ribs, her thighs, the fragile bird-bone rise of her hips, the drift of springy hair, and then with his fingertips the edge of what felt like another mouth, a secret mouth, as moist and open as the one he was kissing.

"Chris. . ." she whispered, but it was more like a sigh.

He felt her breath on his neck, her lips at his ear. Then with a swift, light movement she twisted to make it easier for him, and he slipped into her as smoothly as a swimmer entering the water; and then he was hardly conscious of what was her body and what was his, the morning and the night, his innocence, that welcoming, wet, and silky secret mouth.

PART TWO

seven

Jenny felt different. To her, their love-making had seemed clumsy and swift and a little sad, too, but there was time to learn, and she was moved by his tenderness toward her. She stayed with him on Saturday and spent the night with him, and all manner of things might have been well; but while she was asleep in his arms early on Sunday morning, something happened that fell between them like a sword.

The Oxford police had been concerned for some time at the amount of drug trading in the city, and they had decided to make a dawn raid on everyone they thought might be involved. That included the group living in the squat. In fact, the police were wrong. Although Derek and Ollie smoked marijuana from time to time, they'd never dealt; and Jenny herself had touched no drugs at all since her episode with Tansy. But that wouldn't have made any difference. She would have been swept in with Derek and Ollie and a

71

hundred others, except of course that she wasn't there.

She knew nothing about the raid until she left Rose Hill on Sunday evening to go home. When she turned the corner of the street where her house was, she knew at once that something was wrong. A large sheet of plywood had been nailed across the doorway, and the ground floor windows were boarded up too. There was no point in even trying to get in; she knew exactly what had happened.

Nor was there any sense in going to the police and asking for her things back, her clothes and the few bits and pieces she'd acquired. It would only mean getting dragged into Derek and Ollie's business, and, much as she liked those two, she had no faith in the police. She thought that they'd be bound to say there'd been drugs in her room as well; it was inevitable.

The little money she had and the clothes she needed immediately were with her in her rucksack. The natural thing to do would have been to ring Chris and tell him what had happened, but there was a simple and ludicrous reason why she couldn't: in the time she'd spent with him, which hadn't really been long, she had never learned his surname or his address, and so she had no way of finding out his phone number.

She might have gone to Oxford Entertainment Systems and found him there, but all she knew about the firm he worked for was that it was based somewhere in East Oxford; she had no idea what it was called, or what Chris actually did there. Another thing she could have done was go back to the house in Rose Hill and ask Chris's father, who must have returned by now, for Chris's address or phone number. But she couldn't make herself do that. Despite what Chris had said about him, a father was a father, and she felt too uncomfortable to speak to him, in view of what she'd been doing in his house. A day never went past—in fact, hardly an hour went past—without her own father haunting some corner of her thoughts.

So she didn't speak to Chris. Instead she went to the rented flat of a friend who sometimes worked in the same café, and slept on her floor. She'd find Chris before very long, she thought.

As soon as he finished work on Monday afternoon, Chris got on his bike and raced along the Cowley Road to Jenny's house. It was a hot day, and he stopped to buy a couple of ice-cream pops, intending to take one to her. When he saw the plywood nailed across the doorway, he stopped as if he'd been punched in the heart.

He stood astride his bike, the hot sun beating on his back, and then remembered the ice-cream pops melting in the paper bag. He tore one open automatically, so as not to waste it, and stood there gazing stupidly up at the blank wood, the blank windows.

A little farther down the road a car door opened, and a shirt-sleeved policeman got out. Chris didn't even notice when the man appeared beside him, his expression invisible under his peaked cap and sunglasses.

"Looking for someone?" he said.

Chris had a mouthful of ice cream. He was conscious of the stuff melting down the stick and over his fingers, and felt at a disadvantage.

"Yeah," he said when he'd swallowed. "What's happened?"

"Who were you looking for?"

Then Chris remembered that Jenny and the others had been squatting, that the house wasn't legally theirs. If he said anything about her, he might get her in trouble.

"A friend," he said.

"What's this friend's name?"

"Why? I mean, what's going on? What's happened here?"

"Did your friend live here?"

"Yeah. But—"

"What's your friend's name?"

The ice cream finally dropped off the stick and onto the pavement, splashing a drop or two on the policeman's polished shoe.

"Look, what's going on?" Chris said anxiously. "Why don't you tell me what's happened? Are they all right? Has there been an accident or something?"

The policeman seemed to be sizing him up. Then he took off his sunglasses and said, "Look, son, I'm not trying to be difficult. Was he a good friend of yours, this feller?"

Chris's mind raced. It sounded as if something bad had

happened—but not to Jenny, or the policeman would have said *she*.

"No, just someone I know. His name's Derek."

"Well, your friend was arrested yesterday and charged with selling drugs. Was that what you came here for?"

"What? Drugs?" Chris was gaping with astonishment. "Me? 'Course not!"

"No, naturally," said the policeman, taking out a notebook. "Can I have your name and address?"

"What for?"

"In case your friend needs your help. In case we need to get in touch with you."

Like most people his age, Chris had had little to do with the police, but he feared and mistrusted them. On one occasion earlier that year, he'd been cycling home late with his friend Carl, and two policemen in a car had made them stop and give their names and addresses, and had insisted on checking their bicycles to see if they were marked with their postcodes. Chris remembered feeling frightened and helpless, even though he'd done nothing wrong, and he felt the same now. It simply never occurred to him to give a false name and address; and if it had, he'd have imagined that the truth would be found out, and it would make things worse. So, angry and resentful, he gave his real name and address. The policeman wrote them down.

"What about the others living here?" Chris asked.

"Others? What others?"

"Derek's friends."

"Who might they have been?"

"You want me to give you their names, right? So you can look for them, too?"

The policeman looked at him steadily. "If they're involved, and if you know anything about them, and if you withhold that from the police, then you're involved too, sunshine."

"I just told you my bloody name, and it's not sunshine."

"This is true," said the policeman. "It's a good thing I know you're telling the truth, Chris. I can always tell. Well, now, whoever was living here was doing so illegally. Squatting, in a word. They'd been warned to leave, so they were liable to be arrested for trespassing, in any case. How helpful do you want to be to your friends?"

The meaning was clear: I'm going to tell you nothing, but the more we talk, the more you'll tell me. Chris found himself flushing with anger. He couldn't ask about Jenny without incriminating her.

"Where are they now?" he said.

"In St. Aldate's police station, I expect."

Chris turned to go. He dropped the paper bag with Jenny's ice cream into the nearest trash can, and rode away with his head thudding.

As soon as he got home, and his mother had gone into the garden so he could do it without being overheard, he phoned the police station.

"Hello. I'm trying to find someone. . .she's missing. . ."

He had to give his name and address. Having had time to think, he gave a false one.

"And who's the missing person?"

"Her name's Jenny. Er—this is stupid. I'm sorry, I don't know her surname."

"Where does she live?"

He hesitated. "Somewhere in East Oxford. Off the Cowley Road. I'm not sure exactly. She's about seventeen years old, and she's slim, and she's got short dark hair. Oh, she's white—got a Yorkshire accent."

"How long's she been missing?"

"About. . .twenty-four hours."

"And what's your connection with her? I mean, do you work with her? Is she a friend, or what?"

"She's a friend."

"Girlfriend?"

"Well, yeah."

"You don't know where she lives, you don't know her surname. . . . What, did she not turn up for a date or something?"

Chris felt foolish and bitter. "Yeah, something like that."

"She comes from Yorkshire, you say? Could she have gone home?"

"Well, I suppose she could have."

"Why don't you try there, then? We haven't got much to go on here, have we?"

"No, but. . . .I think she might have been arrested, that's all."

"When?"

"Yesterday."

"What, here in Oxford?"

"Yeah. Possibly."

"Just hang on a minute."

The phone went quiet. A short while later the voice spoke again.

"Nobody of that description has been arrested here, I can tell you that. Would you mind telling me what—"

Chris stopped listening. He put down the phone.

eight

*That evening Mike Fairfax was attending a meeting some-*where, so Chris and his mother had supper together on their own. Instead of eating at the big table in the kitchen, as they did when Mike was there, they had pizza on their laps watching television. Chris was glad that they didn't have to face each other and talk. There was only one thing that was occupying his mind, and he didn't want to talk about that.

His mother was a good-looking woman of forty, whose dark hair and skin led some people to think of her as Middle Eastern, even though she wasn't. She worked as an art teacher in a private school, and from time to time she half-seriously took up pottery, or weaving, or some other craft, and got quite good at it before losing interest. She feared that she was less interesting, less gifted and magnetic than Chris's father, and she was probably right. She suspected that Chris enjoyed his company more than hers, and she was right there too. All in all, she was an unhappy woman, and only Mike Fairfax had saved her from becoming bitter; but now, in love with him, she gave off a glow of contentment that even Chris noticed.

That evening as they sat together in the untidy comfort of their living room, she felt that she'd been neglecting her son and realized that they hadn't even planned a holiday that year. In all the changes that had been taking place, it had simply been forgotten.

"I've just thought!" she said. "We haven't got anything planned."

"What sort of thing?"

"A holiday. I should have thought. . . It just slipped my mind. How *stupid.*"

"Doesn't matter. I don't want to go away in any case."

"Oh, come on, don't be a stick in the mud. We always go away."

"With Dad, yeah."

"Well, things are different. But we should still have a holiday."

"Everything's different. Anyway, Barry Miller needs me full-time. He said so."

"What, forever? It's only a holiday job. Is he *forbidding* you to go away or something?"

"There's nowhere I want to go. Anyway. . ."

He didn't know how to put it. She guessed what he meant, though, and, feeling confident for once, she said, "Anyway what?"

"Well, I mean, who would it be?"

"What d'you mean, who would it be?"

"Well, me and you, or what? You talking about Mike as well?"

"Why not?"

"No reason why not. I'm just saying would he be coming with us?"

"I don't know, Chris. I haven't asked. I only this minute thought about it. I just thought that we hadn't planned a holiday, and I thought you might like to go abroad somewhere, that's all."

He shrugged. "Well, normally. . . I don't know, Mum. I just hadn't sort of reckoned on it."

"Well, wouldn't you like to?"

"No, actually. If you're asking what I *want,* well, what I *want* is to stay here and work for Barry Miller. I don't want to go anywhere."

They were both watching the television rather than each other, though neither could have said what the program was about. She took a careful sip of her wine.

"Would it make a difference if Mike didn't come?" she said.

"No."

There was another pause.

Then Chris said, "Why don't you and Mike go off by yourselves?"

"What? Don't be silly."

"Why's that silly?"

"I'm not leaving you on your own."

"I can cope. I managed all right at Dad's. I managed here, actually, before you met Mike."

"I know, darling. I know you can. It's not that. But I couldn't go off and leave you on your own, absolutely not. I just can't understand why you want to spend all summer working at a boring little job in Cowley."

"Because I like Barry Miller, that's why. And it's not boring. And if you're going to twist this around and make out it's me preventing you from having a holiday, I'm not, okay? I *can* look after myself, and I'm *happy* to look after myself, so if you and Mike want to go off somewhere that's *fine*. That's okay, that's no problem. Just *go*."

The last thing Chris wanted to do for the rest of that evening was sit and watch television. Restless, unhappy, desperate to see Jenny again and hold her safe in his arms, he left the house as soon as he'd stacked the dishwasher, and cruised the warm evening streets on his bicycle, scanning every face, and finding her nowhere. Only when it was completely dark did he turn reluctantly back toward home.

The girl on whose floor Jenny spent Sunday night had left her old job and gone to work in a café that had become popular with the sort of people who liked to be seen drinking fashionable foreign beer and listening to the latest fashionable live music, which that summer was jazz. The café sold calzones and pizza and baked potatoes on cast-iron plates and salad in wooden bowls, and the staff sounded even more aggressively snobbish than the customers.

They needed another waitress, and since Jenny had run out of money, her friend suggested that she come along and meet the manager. He was named Tommy Sanchez. He was in his thirties, stocky and husky-voiced; his long dark hair was tied back in a ponytail. He had the same upper-class background as his staff and customers. Jenny wasn't the sort of girl he normally hired, but he offered her a job starting that Monday night. She knew she was lucky to find one so quickly; she had no choice but to accept.

She was becoming more and more aware of the effect she had on certain kinds of men. They were usually much older than she was, old enough to be her father, and they seemed to sense some quality in her that aroused them. And then they stopped being men and became something like tigers or wolves—bright-eyed, cruel-mouthed, intent not on kindness or friendship or love but on consuming her, destroying her, rending her apart.

Boys and men she liked and trusted, on the other hand, were either those whose interests lay elsewhere, like Derek and Ollie, or those who carried a sort of innocence with them, like Chris. She'd never met anyone quite like him. He was no coward, no weakling, nor was he just ignorant or childish; but there was something clean and unknowing about him, like a pure-hearted inhabitant of some unpolluted culture a long way away. There was nothing more she wanted to do, in the time they spent together at Rose Hill, than to tell him all about her father and how he'd blasted and destroyed her childhood. But at the same time she knew it would shock him; she feared that he would come to see her as she saw herself: corrupt, poisonous, tainted.

And when she met Tommy Sanchez, she recognized him at once for the type she knew, and made up her mind to keep clear of him as much as possible. And to spend all her spare time looking for Chris.

While she did that, he was looking for her. The city of Oxford isn't big enough to get lost in, and it would have been possible for them to meet by chance; but bad luck kept them apart.

For one thing, Jenny was working in the café all evening, which was mainly the time that Chris had to look for her; whereas during the morning and afternoon he was usually at the warehouse or out in the van. Secondly, if she'd been working in any other café he might have gone in for coffee or something to eat, and come across her that way. But the year before, when the place had opened, Chris had gone there looking for a summer job, and Tommy Sanchez had been so unpleasant that he swore he'd never go there again. And, finally, Jenny had to move. She couldn't sleep on her friend's floor forever, and places in Oxford itself were almost impossible to find. Now that she had a steady job she could at least afford a room, even though it wasn't in the city. She found a bed-sitter in

Kidlington, a bus ride to the north, the place where Barry Miller lived; so for much of the time she wasn't even in Oxford.

Their paths did cross. Once they came within a few yards of each other; but the street was crowded with tourists, and they simply walked past, unseeing. And once in the late afternoon, as Jenny was sitting in the hot minibus going down the Banbury Road to work, she saw Chris riding up the other way—grim-faced, intent, and withdrawn. She asked the driver to stop, and jumped out at once, but Chris was too far away to hear her calling, and he didn't look back.

Finally, swallowing her misgivings, telling herself not to be stupid, Jenny went to Rose Hill and rang the bell of Chris's father's house. All she had to do was ask his address, after all.

But there was no one there, and a real estate agent's sign in the front garden said SOLD. Chris's father and Diane had moved out to their cottage near Long Hanborough, and the vacant Rose Hill house had sold quickly. The bell resounded in the empty hallway, and no one answered, and Jenny came away defeated and unhappy.

nine

About ten days after he'd last seen Jenny, Chris was sitting in the warehouse checking through some stage lights that had just come back from hire when Barry Miller came in. The two of them were alone; Dave and Tony were out on a job somewhere. Barry sat down on the bench near Chris and picked up a switch, fiddling with it absently. He looked preoccupied.

"How's the chalet?" said Chris.

"Oh, fine. That infrared thingy hasn't come through yet. Suppose I ought to give 'em a ring. Hey, you done any plastering?"

"Never."

"Joinery? Carpentry?"

"Well, a bit. I can saw straight, put screws and nails in, do simple joints. . . . What sort of thing do you mean?"

"In the chalet. The walls, right, they're just concrete paneling. Well, I want to put studs in—you know, a timber frame along the inside to nail plasterboard to. And put insulation in behind it. Keep the place nice and snug."

"I could do that."

"And maybe a stud partition across one end, with a door in it."

"Yeah," said Chris. "Easy."

"What, on your own?"

"Well, it can't be too hard, can it? Wood's easy stuff. So's plasterboard, probably. I couldn't do proper plaster; I wouldn't try. But I like wood. Yeah, I could do that."

"What about a ceiling?"

"I'm trying to remember the roof. . . . It's corrugated iron, isn't it?"

"Yeah. Corrugated iron over timber beams. Sloping, you know. But I thought I'd have a false ceiling, just to make it look tidier. Nothing fancy. Polystyrene tiles, maybe."

"So you'd want a framework there first. I'd need help for that, I reckon. You can't hold something above your head *and* work on it."

"We could do that together, maybe. But if you want to do the walls, I'll make it worth your while."

"Okay, then," said Chris. "Do you know what materials you want? I mean sizes and quantities? Otherwise we'll have to go there and measure up, work it out. And what about plumbing? You were thinking about that last time."

"Oh, I'll get around to that sometime. No hurry for that. No, listen, the thing is not to speak about that place to anyone at all. Not even Sue or Sean."

"No. I know."

"'Cause, you know, I'm not exaggerating, it could be bloody dangerous."

"What was it all about, then?" Chris said. "This family that's after you. . . . What're you supposed to have done?"

He thought he had the right to ask, since he was being involved in the building of the chalet. Barry looked around carefully and lowered his voice when he answered.

"I mentioned Ireland, didn't I? Northern Ireland. Belfast. I used to work there. . . . I dunno how much I can tell you, but bugger the Official Secrets Act—the whole thing stinks. I was working for the army, right. Special technical operations. Connected with the S.A.S. Not *in* the army but sort of attached. It was all unofficial, you know, deniable. In case anything went wrong, we didn't exist, kind of thing. We were involved with bomb disposal, surveillance, anything electronic.

"Anyway, the point is, there was this paramilitary group. A family named Carson. Protestants. Most of the time we were working against the other lot, the I.R.A.; but this bunch were nutters, honest. Killers. Murderers. We got word they were looking for an explosives expert, some bloke from London. He was an expert on industrial explosives, and he was a bit bent, you know. He'd do anything, sell anything. But he knew how to get his hands on some

Semtex, which the Carsons never used before, it was new to them. They didn't want to blow themselves up.

"Well, what they reckoned—the blokes in charge of our unit—they reckoned they'd intercept the London bloke, 'cause the Carsons had never met him, see; they didn't know what he looked like. They'd keep the real bloke out of the way and get someone to substitute for him. You know, pretend to be him, go and meet the Carsons, and catch 'em red-handed. So they asked for volunteers, and I did it."

Chris was listening half-incredulously. It was the sort of story you saw in TV thrillers. And yet things like that *did* happen, and Barry was telling it in a slow, reluctant, embarrassed way which made it very hard to disbelieve.

"So what happened?" Chris said.

"Well, I pretended to be this explosives expert, which was easy enough. I knew all the technical side. And I set 'em up. Tape recorder, hidden video camera, the lot. Trouble was, there was a fight. There was an ambush. The whole thing went off half-cocked. The R.U.C.—you know, the police—they hadn't been properly briefed, and they stumbled on it, and before we knew what was happening there were bullets flying all over the bloody place. One of the Carsons, Frank, he was jailed. Twenty years. Another one, his brother Billy, he got shot. Their cousin was killed as well. Most of the group was rounded up, and we got Frank and the others on tape, so I suppose they called it a success.

"But there was a third brother, see. Eddie, the youngest.

89

He wasn't involved directly. They had nothing on him at all. He was clean. Except that he was the worst of the lot. He was cold, see, clever. . . . He was a thinker. And *revenge*. . .bloody hell, talk about the Mafia—that's nothing on the Irish. Protestants, Catholics, they're all as bad. So Eddie Carson's out for revenge. And the trouble is, he knew it was me that got Billy killed and Frank banged up for twenty years. As far as Eddie was concerned, I was dead meat.

"So there was nothing for it. Once your cover's busted, that's it, you might as well pack it in. They give me some money, new papers; I changed me name. . . ."

He looked rather shamefaced at this, as if it were cowardly.

"What, your name's not really Miller?" said Chris.

"No. Sean doesn't know, and I'm not sure I'm ever going to tell him. My name's really Springer. Or it was. Legally it's Miller, but, you know. . . . So there it is. That's what it's all about."

Chris had no way of judging how true the story was except his own knowledge of the world, and that (as Jenny had seen) was scanty. But he liked Barry and wanted to believe him, so he put aside any doubts that raised themselves, and tried to imagine the Barry he knew in the company of S.A.S. men and terrorists. Only later did the story begin to feel thin and unlikely, as Chris found the obvious questions to ask; but he couldn't bring it up again. It left Barry seeming smaller, somehow. Granted, you had to stoop to all kinds of things to catch terrorists, but to set them up like that. . .wasn't that a kind of betrayal? And if he'd betrayed someone once, might he not do it again?

The next day Chris had to go out with Dave to take some equipment to a theater group performing in the Oxford Union. This was a large Victorian building in the center of town; it was where the famous Oxford Union debates took place, where undergraduate would-be politicians rubbed shoulders with government ministers and took the first steps on the road to Parliament. Chris had never been inside it before, but Dave was familiar with the place.

"I spoke here once," he said as they unloaded the lighting trees onto the lawn.

"Spoke? What d'you mean?"

"In a debate. I think we lost."

"You? Really? When?"

"When I was an undergraduate. I think it was Lady Antonia Fraser on the opposing side. I can't remember. I was too nervous."

Chris looked at him with new eyes. Dave was thin, shabby, wiry, with immensely long brown hair and a wispy beard, and he moved in a perpetual atmosphere of vague peaceableness, like a hippie.

"Wow," said Chris. "I never thought of you like that."

"Well, it's not exactly a conversational earthshaker, so I don't bother to mention it. I just remembered it, coming here."

The theater group was presenting a summer season of two plays, and they were about to change from one to the other, which was why they needed the new equipment. Chris and Dave carried it in, handed it over to the director, and were about to take out the pieces they no longer needed when Chris heard a voice he recognized.

The confident, arrogant tones came from around the corner of the wide corridor. It was the voice of the young man by the lake, the one named Piers.

Instantly Chris felt his flesh prickle. It was a chemical change; he couldn't help it. The flood of adrenaline suffused his whole nature with fury. The memory of those few minutes by the lake and his passion for Jenny suddenly blazed, and he forgot Dave and the job they were doing and sprang to the corner of the corridor before Piers could vanish.

Piers, dressed with cool summer elegance, was talking to an elderly man and a girl of nineteen or so. He was saying, "Well, yes, of course normally I would. I was actually on my way to Cannes, but these God-awful people turned up, some cousins of Anna's or something, and—"

Chris butted in.

"Are you Piers?"

Piers turned, an expression of astonished contempt on his handsome face.

"That's my name, yes. Who are you?"

"Where's Jenny?"

"I beg your pardon?"

"D'you know where Jenny is?"

"I don't know what you're talking about." Piers turned away, with a smile to the girl, who smiled back nervously.

"Jenny!" Chris said. "Where the hell is she?"

Piers took the girl's arm and began to move away, as if Chris was something embarrassing like a beggar or a drunken vagrant. With a disapproving frown at Chris, the elderly man followed them down the corridor. Chris felt his rage spread like fire on gasoline, to include the building as well, the pompous, oak-lined walls, the portraits of famous ex-presidents, the whole world Piers represented. He sprang after them and seized Piers by the arm, pulling him around.

"Answer me! You know who Jenny is. You know exactly what I'm talking about, so where is she?"

For answer Piers slapped his face.

There was a moment's silence in the corridor. Dave had come to see what was going on; a door had opened, and two faces were looking out; the elderly man and the girl stood frozen. The crack of the slap seemed to hang in the air like a gunshot.

Then Chris flung himself at Piers in the greatest rage he'd ever known. Piers was taller and heavier than he was, and he'd boxed at his public school. In a properly supervised match he'd have knocked Chris out in less than a minute. But no opponent he'd ever faced had come at him intending to kill. Chris did, and a horrified part of his mind was aware of it, but that wasn't enough to hold him back; he was out of control. He was hit hard, more than once, but

93

he didn't feel the blows. He slammed into Piers, smashing him backward and into the wall, and then hammered him down to the floor, his inhibitions blown away. All he heard were those drawling, contemptuous tones by the lake; all he saw was the arrogant lift of Piers's lip; all he felt was the shame of that slap on his cheek. And all the time an image of Jenny, frightened, hiding. . . . He tore at the bigger man like a tiger, and if he could, he would have killed him.

But Dave was there, pulling him away, and the theater director and someone else came to help. The girl was kneeling by Piers, and the elderly man was protesting angrily. . . .

Chris was dumb. The anger was still there, but he was seeing more clearly, and hearing snatches of speech:

"—don't know what he was talking about—"

"—like a mad dog—"

"—fighting over a girl—"

"—this chap hit him first, I saw it—"

"—anything broken?"

"Get out! Go on! Piss off, and don't come back!"

As Dave drove them away, looking concerned, Chris sat trembling in the passenger seat, and began to realize what he'd done, and to feel the damage Piers's blows had inflicted: his lip was cut, a tooth was loose, and he ached all over.

"Wow," said Dave. "I thought you were sort of calm and easygoing. I'd never have expected that sort of operatic rage. That was really quite impressive. What is it, the phase of the moon or something? Does it come over you often?"

"I've never done that before," said Chris carefully, trying not to let his voice shake.

"You reminded me of Barry for a minute. You ever seen him in a rage?"

"No." Shaking his head was painful; he spoke through a half-closed mouth.

"He lost his rag with Tony a few weeks ago, when he bought that shed by the canal. . . ."

Dave paused to negotiate the gap between a bus taking on passengers and a truck coming in the opposite direction. Even through his shame and the remains of his rage and his painful thudding headache, Chris took notice. How did Dave know about the shed if it was supposed to be a secret?

"Why?" he said.

"Oh, Tony was teasing him. He kept referring to the shed as Barry's love nest. Finally Barry flipped his lid and slung a lantern at him. Tony only just ducked in time, I swear it. One of those big Fresnels. . .it would have taken his head off. It smashed to pieces. He hates being teased about his girlfriends, old Barry."

"What girlfriends? I thought he was happily married!"

"Well, so he may be, but he's still giving Sandra one, for a start. Participating in the rites of Venus at the back of the shop. You hadn't noticed? Watch out for it, and you'll see what I mean."

Chris sat silent, sick to his heart. Everyone and everything and everywhere he looked was rotten, corrupt, poisoned to the core.

ten

Jenny was alone. Some days went by without her speaking to anyone except the customers in the café and the other waitresses. Tommy Sanchez usually managed to find a minute or two to talk to her on her own, and she smiled and answered politely, then slipped away to clear a table or take an order before he could touch her.

She continued to look for Chris, but with less and less conviction. She wasn't sure if she loved him, as he'd said he loved her; she didn't think she deserved to love anyone. As for their weekend at Rose Hill, all she had left was a sense she'd never known in waking life and didn't have a name for. In fact, it was goodness; it was the sense of being lapped and bathed in a goodness as fresh as the air in spring. But like all feelings known only in dreams, it had already begun to fade. Everything was fading. The exhilarating freedom of those first days away from home, when she knew she'd never see her father again; the bizarre, disjointed months with Tansy, which at least had been wild fun; the time with Piers, the champagne, the parties—they were dry and dead now, the leaves of another year.

So she looked for Chris, but fatalistically, half-convinced that she'd never see him again.

The house in which she was living belonged to a woman named Gill Petrie. She was in her thirties, with two children under ten, and she was a widow; her husband had died in a motorcycle accident two years before. It wasn't easy for her to go out; she didn't belong to a baby-sitting circle because she couldn't leave her own children to sit with someone else's. It wasn't long before Jenny offered to baby-sit on her free nights, and Gill began to go out a little more.

One day she said to Jenny, "Could you baby-sit tomorrow? It's not actually for me; it's for a friend."

Jenny agreed. There was nothing else to do, and at least she'd be earning a pound or two instead of spending her time compulsively on fruitless bus rides.

She turned up at the address Gill gave her at seven o'clock the next evening. It was a neat, modern little house like a thousand others, and the family was like a thousand others too: pretty, slightly anxious wife, good-humored, bustling husband, shy young son. It was their wedding anniversary; the wife explained. They were going out for a meal, and they wouldn't be back late. There was a snack and some coffee; there was the TV, the phone.

Jenny was puzzled by the wife's anxiety. There was a shadow in the house as if someone were ill, and she couldn't place it. She spent some time talking to Sean, the boy—or rather drawing him out and listening. She hadn't had much to do with children, and she found him delightful. Her landlady Gill's children were still very young, but she could really have a conversation with Sean, once he'd gotten over his shyness.

He was fascinated by science. He had a big star map on the wall of his bedroom, and he told her all about the big bang theory and how the universe was born. She looked down his microscope and saw the leg of a fly. She told him that, no, she didn't really believe in unidentified flying objects, and he told her several different theories about them. He asked if she played chess, and she said no, she didn't know the rules.

"I'll teach you," he said. "It's complicated at first, but you soon get the hang of it."

"It's time for you to go to bed," she said. "I promised your mum."

"Well, can I show you when I'm in bed?"

"Only if you're there in less than ten minutes from now."

He was, so she sat on the bed—not unwillingly—and he set the pieces out on the board between them, with the duvet making it bend at the ridge, and began to explain. She listened with half an ear, asking questions occasionally so that he knew she was still with him; but most of her attention was absorbed by his innocent enthusiasm, his faith in the wonder of things, his untouchedness.

After he'd explained the moves he said, "Shall we have a game now?"

"No, heck, it's too late for that. Anyway, I'm hungry—I want my tea. And I said to your mum that you'd be in bed a long time before now."

"Will you play next time, then?"

"All right, I promise."

"Can I read for a bit?"

"Fifteen minutes."

She watched as he swept the chess pieces into their box, dropped the board on the floor by his bed, and reached up for a book from the shelf above his head. Then—she couldn't help it—she put her arms around him and kissed him. He submitted politely. He smelled of milk, toothpaste, innocence. She kissed him again, helplessly, like someone in love, and saw his eyes widen in surprise. She let go at once.

"Good night, Sean," she said.

He said good night and she left the room, trembling with shame and longing. She knew what she wanted. She wanted to take that little boy's face and press it to her breast. She wanted to kiss him again a hundred times. Desolate with self-hatred, she sat on the edge of the sofa in the last of the evening sunlight and wondered how deep the corruption went that her father had put into her. She was no better than he was; she should never baby-sit again. She should go and live on her own entirely; she shouldn't live at all.

When it was dark, she went to the cheerful little kitchen, made some coffee, and listlessly picked up a biscuit. She didn't really want it. She was deciding whether or not to put it back when the phone rang.

"Hello?" she said.

"Hello," said a man's voice. "Is that Barry Springer's house?"

She had to think before she remembered their surname. "No," she said. "Mr. and Mrs. Miller."

"You're not sure? I heard you hesitate."

"No, I'm sure. You probably got a wrong number."

"Who is this, anyway? Mrs. Springer?"

"What d'you mean?"

"Who am I speaking to?"

"I'm the baby-sitter."

"Ah, I see. He's out, then."

"Well, it's not the same name—"

"Tell him Carson's getting warm. Can you remember that?"

"But who shall I say? And his name's not—"

"Oh, he'll know. Don't forget."

And he put down the phone.

For no reason, Jenny felt cold all over. She poured the coffee and took it into the living room, where she sat watching a James Bond film without moving until the car drew up outside and she heard the key in the door.

"Hello!" said Mrs. Miller. "Everything all right? Sean go to bed on time?"

Jenny got up and went into the kitchen with her. "Yeah, fine. He showed me how to play chess."

"He's always looking for someone to play chess with him. D'you fancy a cup of tea? I always like tea after a meal, and they only did coffee in that place we went to."

She filled the kettle and put three mugs out, bustling about, happily at home in her kitchen.

"Did you have a nice meal?"

"Yes, lovely. . . . Italian. I like Italian; it's my favorite. We'll be all garlic tomorrow. Whereabouts do you work, love?"

She knew Jenny was a waitress. Jenny told her about Tommy Sanchez's café.

"But I don't suppose I'll be there for long," she said. "I don't want to be a waitress forever."

Barry came in, rubbing his hands. "Sean's fast asleep," he said. "What you done to him, eh?"

Jenny glanced at him anxiously, but he'd meant nothing by it. He picked up the biscuit she'd put down earlier and ate it whole.

"Greedy pig," said his wife. "You've just had a huge meal."

"Yeah, it was nice. We'll go there again."

He winked at Jenny. She smiled back. He was easy to like.

As they sat in the living room with their tea Sue said, "What are you going to do when you stop working in the café?"

"I don't know. I've got a friend who says I ought to study. Do A Levels. Go to college. But I don't know what I'd study."

"Oh, you ought to," said Sue. "Really. I never did anything like that till recently, and I'm doing an Open University degree now. It's fantastic! I never thought, you know, a person like me. . . . But it gives you all kinds of new perspectives."

"Yeah. I can see that. I just. . ."

"D'you like kids?" said Barry.

"I never had much to do with them, really. It was nice talking to Sean tonight. He's a lovely boy, he really is."

"He's the king of the world," said Barry proudly.

"You could study to be a teacher," Sue told her. "I thought of doing that when I finish my degree. I'm a school secretary at the moment, but I'm sure I could teach."

Jenny had never thought of teachers as being anything but alien, sullen, hostile failures. The thought of this pretty, pleasant, sensible woman being a teacher made her see all kinds of possibilities for a moment. The world seemed an open and friendly place.

After they'd had their tea, Barry offered to drive her home. She said no, it was only ten minutes' walk, but he insisted. He didn't like the idea of girls out alone at night.

In the car he said, "Is everything all right?"

"What d'you mean?"

"Well, excuse me if I'm out of order, but you just looked so unhappy when we got back."

"Oh!" She didn't know how to respond. "Well. . .no, I suppose it's just my expression. I'm all right."

"You looked tragic. That's the word. Can we get you to sit for Sean again?"

"Yeah. If you want me to. Whenever I'm free."

"And, look, you got any trouble or anything, anything we can help you with, don't wait, you know what I mean? I don't believe in hanging about, me. Nor does Sue. She's a great girl. Talk to anyone. She can't stand in a bus queue without some old girl pouring out her troubles to her. All the kids at school—they go to her instead of the teachers. You can come and talk to her anytime."

"Thanks," Jenny said as they pulled up outside Gill Petrie's house. "Thanks for the lift."

"Pleasure."

He waved through the open window as he drove away, and she remembered that she hadn't told him about the curious phone call from the man who wouldn't leave his name. All in all, it was a strange evening.

eleven

It was becoming clear to Chris what things were good, and what things he was against because they were bad. The loss of Jenny and the fight with Piers, what Dave had told him about Barry—everything was pointing to the conclusion that deceit and betrayal were the worst evil, and truthfulness and fidelity the highest good. If you make a promise, you should keep it. If you break a promise, you don't deserve to live. It made him strong to feel like that: strong but desolate, because in his mind he'd promised to be faithful to Jenny, and she was lost. Still, with the strength came the confidence that he'd find her again. What was right would win. It would have to.

His mother, who was too wrapped in her love for Mike Fairfax to notice Chris's split lip after the fight with Piers, did notice this new mood of his, this grim absolutism; and she commented on it one evening as they sat at supper.

"What's got into you?" she said. "You used to be so tolerant."

"It's the mood of the times," said Mike. He'd taken off his glasses, and his eyes looked mild and moist.

"It's nothing to do with the times, or anything else," said Chris. "What d'you mean, anyway?"

"It's the *Zeitgeist*. The spirit of the age. Fundamentalism."

"Well, he's not as bad as that. . . ." began Chris's mother.

"If something's fundamentally true, it's just as true whatever the age is," said Chris. "It's stupid to say people feel something only because everyone else does. You might as well say you could have a referendum about the force of gravity. If something's true, it's true."

"Well, that in itself is a fundamentalist position," Mike said. "A liberal would say there were more kinds of truth than that. They'd say that what's true is what works, and if one particular belief makes you feel good, then it's true for you. And another belief would be true for someone else."

"Well, they'd be wrong," said Chris. "That's the same as saying nothing's true. It's the same as saying everything's a lie."

"It's the way the world is, Chris."

"It's not! And belief's got nothing to do with making you feel good. Some things you have to believe even if they make you feel terrible."

"Well, whatever turns you on," said Mike, smiling. "Feeling terrible but righteous is just another way of feeling good."

"You *always* do this!" Chris lost his temper and slammed the table, standing up suddenly so that his chair was flung backward. His mother said, "Chris—" and put out her hand, and Mike looked apologetic, but Chris pushed away, blind with anger. "You always—all of you, people like you—all this mush of *feeling good* as if that was the most important thing in the world; as if it didn't matter about truth or justice or honor; as if they were just words to make you *feel good*. . .so you can lie, cheat, deceive your families. None of it matters if only you *feel good* at the end. . . ."

"Chris!" said his mother. "For God's sake!"

He stopped and looked at her. It was a look of blood-chilling contempt. Then he turned and left.

"What's got into him?" said Mike. "Was it something I said?"

"I hope you're not right," said Chris's mother. "About the fundamentalism. I couldn't bear it if he got mixed up with any of that."

They decided that his sudden gloom and flash of temper were due to adolescence, and felt pleased that they were rational and mature and able to keep their passions under control. But in Mike's heart there was a touch of envy, all the same; and as for Chris's mother, it wasn't until she was in bed with Mike that she managed to get out of her mind that expression on her son's face, as cold and absolute as a sword.

A few days after she baby-sat for the Millers, Tommy

Sanchez asked Jenny to come into his office.

It was seven o'clock in the evening of another hot day. Jenny felt her heart sink; she guessed what was going to happen. She edged through the door as Tommy Sanchez, in jeans and espadrilles and a striped T-shirt, opened a bottle of Mexican beer and handed it to her before opening another for himself.

"Sit down," he said from his antique revolving captain's chair. She took the other chair and sat down, like a secretary about to take dictation. The office walls were covered with posters and photographs; jazz records and cassettes littered the desk; a computer and a fax machine stood on a shelf behind him; and a huge Wurlitzer jukebox made it impossible to open the door fully. Feeling numb and helpless, Jenny gazed through the window that overlooked an old green graveyard, long disused, that backed on to the chapel next door.

"How you getting on?" said Tommy.

"Okay, thanks."

"No problems?"

"No. Fine."

"'Cause I worry about you, you know, Jenny."

She looked down and said nothing.

"Drink your beer. It'll get warm."

Obediently she tilted the bottle and swallowed the cold, prickling liquid. Feeling that she ought to say something, she said, "Why do you worry about me?"

Her voice came out much more quietly than she expected. She looked up and saw the same expression she'd seen on other faces: glazed, flushed, intent. He might have been Piers. He might have been her father. She looked away quickly.

"'Cause you look so young," said Tommy. "You look as if you need protecting."

"I don't. I don't need anything."

"Except a job."

The words hung in the air for a moment, and then he leaned forward across the desk.

"Jenny, have a drink with me tonight before you go home. Where d'you live?"

"Kidlington. But—"

"How d'you get home? Bus, or something?"

"The last bus. I'm just in time for it."

"I'll take you home. I'll give you a lift. Let me do that. Go on."

She felt enormously tired, weary to her soul.

"Why don't you just say what you want?" she said.

"I have. I'd like to see you after we close, have a drink, then I'll take you home. That's it."

"That's all? Nothing else?"

"Word of honor."

"I can't be bothered," she said. "I don't believe you. I suppose I should, really. I suppose I should take your word for it. I don't know why I don't—"

He held up his hand. He was so strong and sure of himself, with his heavy clear-cut features, his large dark eyes, and his black eyebrows. She stopped.

"Enough, okay?" he said. "I'm sorry I made the offer. I'm not going to give you any grounds to go whining on about sexual harassment. I don't harass anybody. I don't have to. You don't want to come and have a friendly drink, that's fine; you just say so, I understand. The fact is, I like you. You're a nice girl, attractive girl, intriguing, quiet. I'd like to get to know you, okay?"

She sat looking down and said nothing.

"I don't have to pester my waitresses, Jenny. That's not what this is about."

She looked up, opened her mouth to speak, and then shrugged.

"You look as if you're having a bad time," he said. "I'd like to help. That's all."

"What d'you mean, I look as if I'm having a bad time? What's that look like?"

"Down-in-the-mouth. Unhappy. Not on top of things."

"Not on top of the work."

"You said it, love."

"So this is a threat."

"Nothing of the sort!"

"What you mean is, if I don't. . .do what you want, you'll give me the sack."

"For Christ's sake—"

"Isn't that what you mean?"

"Certainly not!"

His face was rigid with anger. She saw him make an effort and smile.

"Look," he said. "Let's rerun this, okay? We got off on the wrong foot. Pretend we've just come in. It's quiet, nothing doing outside for half an hour or so. We sit down, have a beer. How you doing, Jenny?"

"Okay, thanks," she said.

"You found somewhere to live?"

"Yeah."

"Oh, good. Because you were sleeping on Dorothy's floor, weren't you?"

"Just for a few days."

"It's a long way out, though, isn't it? Kidlington?"

"Not long on the bus."

"How much is the bus fare?"

"One fifty, return."

"That's a lot of money. Christ, that's nine quid a week!"

She shrugged.

"You ought to find somewhere central," he said.

"Then it'd cost more, anyway."

"I know somewhere you could have."

She looked at him, unsure whether he was playing a game or telling the truth, but he looked sincere.

"I've got a flat in Gloucester Green," he explained. "The new development. You know what they call it: Yuppie Towers. I've got two bedrooms; you could have my spare."

There was a glint of a smile in his eyes now, a sort of artless cheeky smile, and she couldn't deny his charm. She twisted her lips to stop herself from smiling too.

"I mean, I'm being straight up, aren't I?" he said. "I'd like to get to know you. No point in being shy about it. I'm not going to hassle you, but you can't expect me to stop trying. You got a boyfriend?"

She said nothing.

"'Course you have," he went on. "Half a dozen. Never mind them. *I'm* going to have you, Jenny. I want you."

"D'you always get what you want?"

"No, that's what makes it fun. You can never tell. Anyway, think about it."

"About what?"

"About my spare room. I mean it. It's true. You could come and see it tonight, move in over the weekend. Why don't you? Think about it. Don't give me an answer now. We'll talk later."

He got up and opened the door for her. She went back to the front of the café and worked for an hour or so, passively, not thinking about it, just letting it sort itself out in her mind, until she knew what she had to do.

At the end of the evening she found Tommy and said, "You know what you said earlier?"

"You changed your mind?"

They were standing in the dark, hot little corridor between the office and the kitchen. There were people around, but they were busy, and it was easy to talk intimately without being overheard.

"Listen," she said, and obediently he leaned closer. She marveled at how easily these dangerous beings did what they were told. "My landlady, right. She'll want a week's notice for my room—you know, a week's rent. I couldn't just walk out without giving her that; it wouldn't be fair. But I've got nothing left of this week's wages. If you let me have what I've earned up to today, okay; I can pay her now, and I'll feel better about it. And then. . ."

She looked up at at him, then down again. It had worked. He pulled a roll of notes out of his pocket and handed over the money she'd earned, and an extra ten-pound note.

"No problem," he said. "What about that drink?"

"Not now. Tomorrow. I'm not feeling too well just at the moment. But thanks."

Acting to her fingertips, she touched his wrist briefly and smiled before turning to go. He didn't suspect a thing.

If she'd intended to defraud him of a really large amount of money, it would have been just as easy. Of course, she wasn't defrauding him at all, but she knew that if she'd simply said she was leaving, she wouldn't have gotten the wages he owed her. As it was, she had to go without her share of the tips; but the extra ten pounds partly made up for that.

However, she now had only enough money for a week or so. The whole dreary round of signing on and job searching lay ahead, and if she failed to find anything, she'd have to leave Gill Petrie's house and drift back to the squalor of night shelters and vagrancy.

She'd almost given up hope of finding Chris.

But as she got off the bus in Kidlington one afternoon, footsore from walking from shops who didn't want her to offices who'd filled the vacancy to hotels who wanted someone with experience, a car drew up beside her and a voice called, "Hey! Jenny!"

It was Barry Miller, Sean's father. She said hello, and he opened the door.

"Give you a lift home?" he said.

"It's only around the corner!"

"Never mind, hop in."

He was so different from Tommy Sanchez, so cheerful and open, and so unlike the miserable faces that had been rejecting her all afternoon, that she felt better just for being in his company.

"Tired?" he said.

"It's so hot. I've been looking for a job."

"No luck?"

"Nothing."

"I wish I had something to offer."

"No, really, I'll find something. Oh! I should have told you the other night! There was this phone call. . . ."

She told him as much as she could remember. The effect was startling. He was tanned and happy-looking, but the color left his face and he seemed to age ten years in a moment. He pulled over to the side of the road and made her try to recall everything.

"What's it all about?" she said.

"You haven't said anything to Sue?"

"No, I only just remembered it. I'm sorry, I should've thought earlier."

"I hope to God he hasn't been frightening her. . . . "

He sat drumming his fingers on the steering wheel, staring unseeing through the windshield. Then he said, "Listen, have you got half an hour? I want to show you something."

"Yeah, okay. But what's it all about?"

"There's a man who wants to kill me," said Barry, putting the car into gear.

He turned around as if to drive back toward Oxford, but took a different turn before they entered the city. Jenny sat with his last words echoing in her mind. Could she believe something that melodramatic? But it was clear that he did.

"Who's this man?" she said.

"He's named Carson. God knows how he's found out where I am. See, I used to be mixed up with this family down South London, Carson and his two brothers. Well, I say mixed up—I didn't have nothing to do with 'em, really. They were bad, they really were. Drugs, girls, clubs. . .they were running the place. Protection rackets. . .you know, you pay us a hundred quid a week, or we'll smash your shop up. And they did, too. And they killed. . . . There was another gang, at least, not a proper gang, not like the Mafia or something, but they were fighting over who was going to run the rackets, you know? In the end the Carsons got the two blokes in charge of the opposition and took 'em to this garage, this little lockup place, and tied 'em up. Then they

114

cut their throats and hung 'em up like animals in the butcher's. They didn't find 'em for a week. . . . 'Course, that was a warning, see. You cooperate with us, or you end up bleeding to death on a hook."

He stopped to concentrate on the traffic at the big junction by the motel. Jenny looked at him and saw him grim-faced, pale, tense.

The car moved out into the stream of traffic and he went on: "I had this business down there. Electrician. Mostly contract work, but I got this little shop. I had plans; I was going to build up the retail side. I mean, I knew what people wanted. I had it all planned.

"And then they come to me for money. You know, pay up or get smashed. And I said no. I wasn't being heroic or nothing; I just said no, no way, I wasn't having it. I knew there'd be trouble, but you can't let people like that run your life. And two or three of the other traders nearby, they heard, and they come in with me. We'd protect ourselves. We agreed that there'd always be one of us on watch, and we had CB radios, baseball bats to fight with. . . . Funny, it never occurred to us to go to the police. You don't do that where I come from. You settle things yourself.

"And one night the Carsons came. They had Molotov cocktails, they were going to gut the place. They weren't half-surprised when we come charging out with the baseball bats. . . . I mean, we was scared all right, you know what I mean? These were killers. We all knew who'd done that cutthroat job in the lockup; everyone knew. But, you know, you can push someone so far. . . . We'd just had enough. We were standing up to fight.

"Only we hadn't banked on one of those bloody fool Carsons having a gun. And he panicked and shot my mate, the Pakistani bloke from the grocer's next door. 'Course someone heard and phoned the police, and before they could get away—'cause we were still fighting, see—there was sirens going, lights flashing, and old Mohammed lying dead in the gutter, the Carsons surrounded. . . . Gawd, even at the time I couldn't believe it; it was like *Miami Vice* or something."

They were turning down toward Wolvercote. It wasn't a part of Oxford that Jenny knew, and she was puzzled when Barry turned the car onto a narrow track between trees.

"Where are we going?" she said.

"My chalet. We'll be there in a minute. Where was I? . . . Oh, the fight, yeah, the shoot-out. Well, it was that that broke the Carsons' power, really. I mean, caught red-handed, smoking gun, all that. . . . We were all taken in, the lot of us, and it all come out in court. There was nothing they could pin on us; we was only defending ourselves. The two older Carsons got sent down for life. The cutthroat business—they nailed 'em for that, too. But the youngest brother, Eddie, he never got charged with nothing. He kept his nose clean. He was never involved in any of the rackets, any of the violence, nothing. But he was the worst of the lot.

"And. . .well, he knew I'd organized it, the resistance.

And I knew he'd be looking for revenge. I'd've stuck it out, faced him, but it was the thought of Sue and Sean. . . . The police said they couldn't protect us. It'd mean twenty-four hours a day, and they just couldn't spare the manpower. Anyway, he was too canny to make a direct threat."

The car came to a halt under the trees. There was a little clearing off to the right, where a number of huts stood, looking like an abandoned mining camp in the American backwoods.

Barry opened the door and got out.

"Come and have a look," he said. "Just over here."

She followed him through the green shady clearing, which was dappled with sunlight but cooler by far than the hot roads she'd been tramping all day. He stopped at the door of the most solid-looking hut and unlocked it, throwing it open with a flourish.

"Fancy a drink?" he said. "Ice-cold Coke, how's that?"

It was a proper little house. She'd been expecting something rough and dirty, but the floor was covered in clean vinyl, the walls were plasterboarded, and part of the space had been partitioned off as a kitchen, with a stainless steel sink, a microwave oven, and a fridge. The kitchen partition hadn't yet been plasterboarded, and it stood like a naked grid of rough timber; otherwise the building work was complete. It was furnished, too: there was a bed with a mattress and duvet, a table and two chairs, a chest of drawers, a portable TV set on a low stand. Everything had a shiny, unused look. On the table lay a Swiss army knife and a set of plastic curtain rods still in their wrapper.

"What's it for?" she said. "You going to live here?"

He gave her a can of Coca-Cola frosted with chill.

"Smart, eh? No, it's not for living in. It's for *looking* as if it's lived in."

The look on his face as he lifted his drink to his lips was one of boyish pleasure in his own guile.

"You'll have to explain," she said.

"It's a trap, see? What I'm going to do, I'm going to lure Carson here, let him think I'm hiding here. Make it look lived in. So he comes here to look for me, only I'm not here. Right, he thinks. I'll wait for him. I know the way his mind works, see. He'd love it. He'd love to sit here for hours just waiting in the dark, and then I'd come in and turn on the light and he'd say 'Hello, Barry, you bastard,' and *bam, bam, bam*, put some bullets in me. He'd love it.

"Only what's really going to happen is the place is going to be surrounded by police, and they'll catch him with his gun in his hand, and that's his goose cooked. What d'you reckon? Is that smart, or what?"

This plan, another impromptu fantasy, of course, and quite different from the one he'd told to Chris, sounded implausible to Jenny. The idea of dozens of policemen creeping through the bushes was enough to make her lips twitch, but she controlled the smile and sipped her Coke. However, there was clearly something behind it all; that phone call had been real, and so had the way he'd gone pale when she'd told him about it. You couldn't fake things like that.

"Well, yeah," she said, aware that he was waiting for a response. "When's he going to turn up, d'you reckon?"

"Not for a while yet. That phone call. . .did he say anything else?"

"No. Just what I told you."

"Don't matter. I know who it was. Well, Carson might find his way to the firm, but he won't find his way *here* till I'm good and ready. Got to lay the trap properly. . . . Here, did you say you were looking for a job?"

"That's right."

"Want to earn a few quid?"

"Yeah!"

"How about finishing off this place? Not the plasterboard; I'll see to that. But I got no time to paint it, put up curtains, that kind of thing. See, it needs curtain rods over the windows. Dead easy—screw 'em in, it's all wood. And the plasterboard needs wallpapering. You ever put up wallpaper?"

"No," she said, smiling at the idea. "I could probably paint it all right, though."

"Paint. . .yeah, why not. It'll need a good few coats. White, I reckon. One of them soft whites, you know, with a bit of yellow or cream in it. Silk emulsion. Yeah, that'll do. How d'you feel about tackling that?"

"Yeah. Fine. I got nothing else to do."

"Start tomorrow?"

"Sure. Anytime."

"Right. Smashing. That'll be brilliant. I'll get a spare key for you, and I'll fetch over the paint and brushes and stuff first thing tomorrow. Lovely job. . ."

They agreed how long it was likely to take, and what he'd pay her, and then they finished their drinks and got ready to leave. It was a beautiful evening; the great heat of the day was beginning to recede, and the clearing outside the shed was dappled with rich greens and browns and golds as the sun slanted in through the younger trees by the canal. As the two of them left the shed and stood while Barry locked the door, Jenny felt a premonition of absurd happiness, as if she were seeing the end of a romantic comedy: she would be working in the shed, brush in hand, and by some extraordinary coincidence, some far-fetched twist of plot, the door would open and there would be Chris. And everything would end happily.

Instead, something else happened. The Swiss army knife Jenny had seen on the table was Chris's, and, having remembered that he'd left it in the shed, he was on his way to get it; and at the very moment when Jenny and Barry came out of the shed, Chris turned into the clearing and saw them. His mood was darker and more savage than ever before. He was ready to believe the worst of everyone and everything, and in that moment he thought he saw it: an older man, bathed in satisfaction, preening himself in the glow of sexual conquest. And Jenny. . .whether she looked like a victim or a willing partner he couldn't tell, because his vision was suddenly splintered with childish tears.

He turned away and left before they saw him.

PART THREE

twelve

As he lay awake that night, Chris told himself over and over again that he shouldn't have turned away—that it was cowardly, it was dishonest, he should have confronted them directly. It was bitter to feel that only a short time ago he'd have done it without hesitation, as he'd confronted Piers. But he'd been mistaken then, and bad luck made him wary.

So his mind divided itself against him. He scorned himself and pitied himself, condemned himself and excused himself, and it was a wretched night. In the end he decided that since his instinct for direct, honest confrontation had unaccountably failed him, he would have to be direct and honest by force of will and confront Barry in the morning. As the sky lightened into gray around the curtains and the birds in the garden began their heartless chorus, Chris finally drifted into an exhausted sleep.

Both his mother and Mike Fairfax noticed his appearance at breakfast, but neither of them dared to mention it till he'd left the house. Then she said to Mike that she thought her son looked as if he'd been sentenced to death.

He laughed briefly and said, "That's odd. I was thinking something similar, but not quite that. I thought he looked like an executioner's apprentice on his first morning at work."

She made a face. "That's a bit grim."

"What's up with him? Do you know?"

"He doesn't say anything. Is that adolescence?"

"Probably. Still, that's not a fatal condition, as far as I know. Perhaps he's in love."

Chris hadn't worked out what he was going to say yet, but he didn't want to wait, so instead of going to the warehouse, he called in first at the shop in the Cowley Road. But the van wasn't there, and neither was Barry. Sandra, getting the shop ready, didn't know where he was.

"But he normally comes in today, doesn't he?" said Chris.

"Oh, yeah. He normally gets in early, too, before me. In fact, he's got to be in before half past nine because there's a rep coming."

Sandra was a pleasant, plump woman in her twenties, with ginger hair and freckles. Since hearing what Dave had said about her and Barry, Chris had looked at her with some curiosity, but without noticing anything between her and her boss other than the sort of friendly, energetic enthusiasm Barry inspired in many people.

"So. . .he's probably at the warehouse, then. Okay. Listen, Sandra, have you ever seen a girl about with him, about my age, slim, short dark hair?"

She shook her head. "Who is she?"

"A girl named Jenny. I met her at this party and then I lost touch with her, and I thought I saw her with him yesterday."

"Why don't you ask him?"

"I was going to. . . . Well, I'll probably see him later. Ta-ta."

"See you," she said, placidly filling the till.

As he cycled up the Cowley Road, Chris thought that if it was true that Sandra was having an affair with Barry, she would have seemed jealous when he'd told her about him and Jenny; but it hadn't affected her at all. Perhaps she thought Jenny was too young to matter. Or perhaps there wasn't anything between her and Barry. Or perhaps she was just naturally calm. Or perhaps she was seething with vengeful jealousy and happened to be good at concealing it. The trouble with the state of mind he'd gotten into was that it didn't let him trust anything or anyone. Suspicion, mistrust, believing the worst of people. . .it was horrible.

The warehouse was a building in a yard off a side street where a number of small businesses had established themselves; there was a central heating engineer, for example, and a furniture restorer, and a man who made radiators for vintage cars. Chris was familiar with the street by this time;

he knew a number of the workers by sight and recognized the vehicles that were usually parked there.

So the white Mercedes that was parked across the road from the entrance to Barry's yard stood out as being unusual. There was someone in it, and as Chris slowed down to turn into the yard, the man called to him.

"Excuse me!"

Chris stopped, straddling the bike, and turned it around to pedal back to the car.

"Yeah?"

The man in the car seemed to be in his late thirties, about the same age as Barry. He was dressed in a dark business suit with a striped tie, and he wore glasses. "D'you know a man named Barry Miller?" he said.

"I work for him."

"Is he around, d'you know, by any chance?"

"Well, he should be. . ." Chris looked into the yard. The big van was there, and he saw Tony unlocking the warehouse door, but Barry's smaller van was not in its usual place by the office window. "No, he doesn't seem to be around this morning."

"There's a shop somewhere, isn't there?"

"Yeah, down the Cowley Road. But he's not there, either. I've just come from there."

The man looked like an insurance salesman, Chris thought, but then he wouldn't have been driving a Mercedes; or a merchant banker, but then he wouldn't be calling on Oxford Entertainment Systems. He had a mild, scholarly expression, so he might have been an academic or a lawyer, perhaps, except that his voice didn't seem to fit that picture, being harsh and strongly London-accented. Chris couldn't place him at all. Some sort of property developer who wanted to have a lavish party organized for his new country home? A businessman who wanted to buy Barry Miller out?

"Hmm. . ." The man tapped his fingers on the steering wheel. "Look, are you supposed to be at work? Have you got a minute or two for a chat?"

"Well, yeah, I should be there now. Let me just go and tell them I've arrived, okay?"

"Sure. Of course."

Chris put his bike in its usual place inside the warehouse and said hello to Tony.

"You seen Barry this morning?" said Tony.

"No. There's this bloke—"

"What, in the Mercedes? He was here yesterday."

"He wants to see me for a minute."

"All right. No hurry. When you've finished, look, there's these lanterns from the wedding disco; they're all buggered. I dunno what they were doing—spraying champagne, I shouldn't wonder. Can you wash 'em all and check the lamps? Make a note of any broken ones, and we'll charge 'em."

It was a normal sort of job; Chris guessed it would take half an hour or so. He went out again to the white Mercedes. The driver beckoned him around to the passenger side and leaned across to open the door. Chris hesitated.

"I've got a job to do," he said.

"Won't take long. But I don't want to talk here. I'll tell you the reason in a minute."

Chris got in, and the driver started the car and began to drive away. The engine was deathly quiet. The car was so well insulated that Chris felt entirely shut away from the rest of the world, so that they moved through the sunny streets in air-conditioned isolation.

The man drove along the Cowley Road for a little way, turned into a side street, and parked outside a row of semi-detached houses.

"What's this all about?" said Chris. "If you want Barry, he's probably in the shop now. He's got to be there at half past nine because there's a rep going to call."

"I appreciate your taking time away from your work. You're not going to lose by it, are you? They won't deduct anything from your pay?"

"No, it's not that, but I mean there's work to be done, you know?"

"Of course, yes, I understand. I won't keep you long. Now, how well do you know Barry Miller?"

"Well, I've been working for him for a few weeks."

"It's not a permanent job, is it? I mean, you're a student, aren't you?"

"Well, Sixth Form, yeah. It's a holiday job."

"Would you mind telling me your name?"

128

Chris hesitated. This was all strange and disorienting. The man saw his doubt.

"I'd better tell you my interest. I should have done that to start with, I'm sorry. My name's Fletcher. I'm a police officer—detective inspector. And you're. . . ?"

"Chris Marshall."

"Right. Chris. Now this is all very awkward. Your boss Barry Miller might, or might not, I don't know, be able to help me in an inquiry I'm making about something slightly tricky. I'm wary of approaching him directly, because he's likely to mistake the nature of the inquiry. . . . You see what I mean?"

"He'll think you're after him?"

"You got it."

"Is it this Irish business?"

"You got it. Look, you want to get back to work, and I don't want to get you into trouble. I'll drive you back there now, but could you give me half an hour or so at lunchtime? When d'you have your lunch?"

"One o'clock, usually."

"What d'you do, packed lunch?"

"Yeah."

"Would you mind if we had a chat?"

"Well. . .as long as. . .yeah, well, all right."

"That's great. Smashing. Now as far as I remember, there's a parking lot off the next road, behind the supermarket. You bring your lunch along there, and I'll see you, what, about five past one, ten past?"

"Okay. Look, I ought to be—"

"Sure. I'll run you back."

The quiet surge of power, the cool air, the silence of the streets outside: you were cut off from the world all right in a car like this, Chris thought. Not like a bike, where you were part of the street, at one with everyone else's sound and movement. In the white Mercedes you were different.

Barry didn't appear in the warehouse all morning, but then they hadn't expected him to. Tony didn't seem at all interested in Mr. Fletcher, and Chris didn't volunteer anything. There was plenty to do; after he'd cleaned the lights from the wedding disco and replaced the broken bulbs, Chris stacked them neatly away and then checked the clip outside the office, where they hung up the order slips waiting to be filled. Sometimes the phone would ring. They had a democratic system: whoever was closest would answer it.

When it rang at eleven o'clock, that person was Chris. Dave and Tony had gone out with a delivery, so he was on his own anyway. He went into the hot little office and picked up the phone.

"Hello, Oxford Entertainment Systems."

"Chris. Wotcher. Barry here. Listen, is Dave around?"

"No, they're both out at Marston—that pub job."

"Oh, right. Look, can you ask Dave when he gets back to pop around to Lasky's and get a five-liter can of silk emulsion paint. I think there's one called 'buttercup white' or summing."

"Buttercups are yellow."

"Yeah, you know what I mean. White with a hint of yellow. And a couple of brushes. Got that?"

"Five-liter can, two brushes—"

"And bring 'em along to the shop. Tell him to sign for 'em."

"Okay."

"Oh, and listen. . .anyone there?"

Chris caught the conspiratorial tone and found himself looking around, though he knew he was alone.

"No," he said. "Just me."

"Look, you know that business I told you about? The Irish business?"

"Yeah, I remember."

"Well, I've had a tip-off. It's coming to a head. Carson's found out I'm in Oxford, but he don't know where just yet. Anytime now I'm going to send Sue and Sean back to her mum's and then I'll go underground. I'm relying on you, Chris. There's no one else knows about the chalet."

Not much, thought Chris bitterly.

"Yeah, well," he said.

"We'll fix up some kind of system. Messages, you know. CB radio, maybe. Just till I sort Carson out. I had this beautiful idea. . . . Look, I gotta go. Don't forget that paint. And listen, Chris, when this is all over, I got brilliant plans. The way you done that joinery in the chalet, beautiful, smashing. It give me an idea, right, for scenery—look, I'll tell you later. Watch out, okay? Keep your eyes peeled."

"I will, yeah."

"Lovely job," said Barry, and rang off.

Chris put back the phone slowly. He'd done it again; he'd run away from asking Barry about Jenny. True, Barry had hardly given him a chance, but you had to make chances, not wait for them.

Next time, he thought.

The white Mercedes was parked in the only patch of shade in the parking lot. Fletcher waved to Chris through the open window.

"Glad you could make it," he said, switching off the radio news. "Have a seat."

Chris sat in the front passenger seat, leaving the door open beside him. Fletcher was eating a sandwich and drinking from a small bottle of mineral water. He offered another unopened one to Chris, who took it.

"You're probably wondering," said Fletcher, "if I'm a policeman, why this isn't a police car, why I'm not in uniform, why this whole thing is so unorthodox. Well, having thought about it carefully, I'm going to tell you. You might have guessed, actually. Have you heard of the Special Branch?"

"That's politics, isn't it?" said Chris.

"Security in general. Particularly as regards terrorism."

Chris tried to work out what all this meant for him. He didn't trust the police, didn't feel that they were on his side; and as for whether it was normal for an officer from the shadowy Special Branch to go about his duties like this, he had no idea. He wondered if he ought to ask for proof; didn't they have to carry some kind of identification? But Chris wouldn't have known what that looked like anyway, far less be able to tell whether it was forged. He had to go on feelings. Did he trust this man or not?

He turned to look into Fletcher's eyes. The man was watching him patiently. How difficult it was to read appearances! They weren't like words; you couldn't say that gray eyes meant honesty, or thin lips meant meanness, or glasses meant respectability. Fletcher's face looked back at Chris's, and Chris understood nothing at all. It was as if the man were wearing some incredibly detailed, immaculately finished mask.

The mask smiled. Chris turned away and unwrapped the ham roll he'd made for his lunch.

"You said something about Ireland," Fletcher said. "Barry Miller had told you something about Ireland. Was that it?"

"I'm trying to remember," Chris said. This was one of the most difficult positions he'd ever been in. Had Barry done something wrong? And if he had, was it right to tell Fletcher about it? It might be Chris's own anger about Jenny that made him want to do it, and not his knowledge of what was right. On the other hand, Fletcher might not be going to arrest Barry but to seek his help. What the hell should he do?

Fletcher must have sensed his doubts. He drummed his fingers lightly on the steering wheel, as if he'd made a decision.

"Look, Chris, you know Barry Miller. He's your boss; he might be your friend. You're worried about talking to me because it might mean betraying him in some way. Am I right?"

"Yes."

"Well, I understand that completely. It does you credit. Does him credit, actually, too. Can you just agree to answer the questions I put to you? Only the ones you feel happy about. Any question you don't want to answer, that's fine by me. And in return you can ask me what you like, and I'll give you an honest answer. If there's anything I can't tell you because of security—the Official Secrets Act—I'll make that clear. How's that?"

"Yeah. Okay. That's fair."

"Good. D'you know where he lives?"

Chris hesitated. "Yes, in Kidlington."

"D'you know the address?"

"I've been there, but I can't remember it."

"Okay. Now, this business about Ireland. Can you remember what he told you?"

"Can you tell me what his real name is?" said Chris.

"Well, Miller *is* his real name, because he changed it by deed poll. But before that he was called Springer."

Chris felt a strange sensation, as if a corner of his mental landscape had settled in a rockfall, altering the shape of things in a small but significant way. It meant that Fletcher was telling the truth.

"Yeah, that's what he told me," he said. "About

Ireland. . . . He said he'd been attached to the army there, in Belfast. He wasn't very clear about it. He sort of hinted at the S.A.S., I thought. Underground work, that sort of thing. He'd helped to break up this paramilitary gang, and one of the family was still after him, a man named Carson. . . Protestant. That's one of the things I didn't understand. I thought the British army and the Protestants were sort of on the same side."

"No. It's not as simple as that."

"Well, no. I half realized that. Anyway, the point is that this man Carson is still after him—that's why he changed his name."

"Ah. He didn't say anything else about Ireland in particular?"

"No. Just a lot of hints. Why? What *was* he doing there?"

Fletcher scratched his head. "I'm afraid he's told you a pack of lies," he said. "For a start, he had nothing to do with the army, let alone the S.A.S. In the second place, he was on the other side altogether."

"What, the I.R.A.? Barry?"

"Well, this is where we start touching what's classified. I don't know if you've heard of an organization called the I.N.L.A.? The Irish National Liberation Army?"

"Yeah, I've heard of it. They're a sort of more extreme I.R.A."

"That's it."

"And you're saying Barry was a member?"

"I'm not *saying* it. . ."

Chris sat silent for a few seconds.

"Why are you telling me this?" he said. "Are you going to arrest him or something? I just can't see what you're after. He's not hard to find. I mean, Christ, he's in the shop now if you want to arrest him. . . . But I can't believe it. Barry Miller? He's not like that. It's crazy. Surely. . ."

Fletcher nodded slowly. He looked tired, wise, understanding.

"That's how they've managed to succeed," he said. "By building on the trust of people who don't know the truth about them. I don't blame you for being taken in. He's a past master. But you think, now. Has he always told you the truth? Do you *know* for a fact that he's a hundred percent reliable? Isn't there *some* doubt in your mind about him?"

Chris said nothing. He looked down at the carpeted floor.

"I've met his wife and his son," he said, a little desperately. "They're good people. *Barry's* a good man sometimes. If you saw him at home . . ."

"It's hard to understand," Fletcher said gently, "but there are some people who can live two separate lives. I've never seen his family, but I'm sure you're right about them. And I'd be prepared to bet that they know as little as you do about the other part of his life. His wife might wonder occasionally, but he'll tell her a pack of lies. Or else she won't ask; she'll keep her worries to herself."

He drank from the bottle of mineral water. Another little

rockfall happened in Chris's mind; because almost the first thing he'd noticed about Sue, after thinking how nice she was, was the faint air of shadowed anxiety that never quite went away. It was exactly as Fletcher had described.

Fletcher put down the bottle, screwing the cap on tightly.

"Look," he said. "I'm going to trust you. I suppose I really should make you sign the Official Secrets Act or something, but you're an intelligent young man. Barry Springer, or Miller, or Daly—yes, he's called Daly too, Michael Daly—is, or was, a supergrass, an informer. He was an I.N.L.A. member for some time, and then he turned himself in. Gave the Special Branch a lot of information about his former associates. He was an expert on explosives. They used to use car bombs in those days. Nowadays, with Semtex—you've heard of Semtex?—which is much more powerful, you don't need such a large amount to make a lethal blast. But those explosives they used to make out of fertilizer—well, a thousand-pound bomb was nothing unusual. That's as much as five heavy adults. Can't leave that in a paper bag; hence the car bomb, you see. Your man Miller, though, he was a wizard with explosives and electronics. He could conjure an explosion out of a bag of sugar."

Chris's head was ringing. He'd remembered Barry's words at the ball on the night he'd met Jenny: *You don't need much powder for a socking great bang.* . . . Hardly knowing what he was doing, he got out of the open door and walked up and down beside the car, holding his fists to his head. No, it was too much; it was impossible. Fletcher was fooling him.

He stopped and bent down to look in at the man. Fletcher was facing him with that same reluctant, tired sorrow, and Chris knew that it was all true, every word.

His heart like lead, he got back in the car. He twisted the top off the bottle of mineral water and put it to his lips. It frothed unpleasantly in his mouth, and he swallowed only a little.

"All right," he said. "Sorry. This is a shock."

"Of course," said Fletcher. "I'll go on. We know that Miller was directly responsible for at least eleven deaths. Mainly soldiers and policemen. We also think he blew up an entire family—father, mother, two small children. That's the sort of man he is. Killing is no problem for him.

"Now the point is, as I said, he became a double agent. In return for immunity from prosecution, he passed on to us a good deal of valuable information; I can't deny it. An entire active unit of the I.N.L.A. was rounded up, and—oh, a lot of information. And it's a standard sort of deal: Springer, or Daly, was given a new identity, papers, money, and he came over here to start a new life as Barry Miller. It wasn't too hard for him, actually. He was brought up in London; he doesn't sound like an Irishman, does he? I don't know how you feel about people like that escaping punishment. It's a dirty world, Chris. I suppose you need dirty people to. . . . Anyway."

He sighed.

"Who's this Carson?" Chris said. "He keeps going on about him."

"The brother of the man whose family was killed. But he's not important; he's just a wild man. He's all mouth. Miller's in no danger from Carson. No, the reason I'm here is nothing to do with that. We discovered—I can't tell you how—we discovered that Miller had never really turned at all. Oh, the information he'd given us had been good, no problem there; he'd genuinely delivered. But they were playing a deeper game. Miller and the I.N.L.A. were aiming all the time to set him up precisely where he is now. They've got a new campaign planned: soft targets in the south of England—the homes of politicians, senior army officers, civil servants, policemen and their families. It's started already. You've probably heard about some of it on the news. And here he is with access to electronic equipment, a perfect cover, right in the heart of England."

No, Chris thought. No, no, it's not true at all, it's impossible. Barry was selling make-up and hiring stage lights, not making bombs; he wasn't evil; he was just a liar. And this was a dream.

He looked at the ham roll he'd taken a bite from. He didn't feel like eating any more of it; he put it back in the plastic box and closed the lid. Fletcher felt in a paper bag beside him on the floor.

"Fancy an apple?" he said.

An apple would be easier to swallow, Chris thought. He took it with a nod. "Why are you telling me all this?"

139

"Because I want your help."

"*My* help? To do what?"

"Chris, I know he's got a hideout somewhere. And I know you've been helping him with a spot of building."

"How d'you know that?"

"Ah, well. You remember our agreement; I can't tell you how I know that. Security. I'm sorry."

"Security? What's that mean? Wiretapping or something?"

"I'm sorry. I can't say."

Chris's face twisted in a spasm of disgust. This whole thing was revolting. A moral stench seemed to be filling the whole car, in spite of the open doors and the air freshener. Fletcher seemed to sense what he was thinking.

"You believe in democracy, Chris. I know that."

"Yeah. That's why I find all this. . .so foul. What he's doing, yeah, of course; but what you're doing too. Don't you see that?"

"Mmm." Fletcher nodded sadly, took the top off the bottle, then put it back without drinking. "Yes, I do. But democracy has a price. It doesn't come free. The price of freedom is eternal vigilance, as someone said. And the price of democracy for" —he waved his hand, indicating the rest of the city—"for everyone out there is that a few people, a very few, have to work *un*democratically. You see, Barry Miller doesn't want democracy, so he tries to subvert it. I don't mean just argue against it. We don't mind political argument; that's what democracy means. But Barry

140

Springer, Barry Miller, Michael Daly, that's not his game at all. He's playing a different game, where you don't stand up and ask for votes, you creep about in the dark and leave bombs to kill people. Innocent people. Women and children. He's done it, Chris. He's planning to do it again."

Chris said nothing. He sat still, feeling sickened, knowing that Fletcher was watching him. The man went on: "So there's precious little point in me, people doing this sort of job, going about it in a democratic way, asking for votes. *He* doesn't ask for votes before he plants a bomb. *Put an X in the box if you want me to kill this mum and two kids. . . .* And it's no good us fighting clean while these people are fighting dirty, because that would mean we'd lose. Everyone'd lose. And to my mind, that's unthinkable. That's why I'm a policeman, you see, Chris, and that's why I'm proud to work for the Special Branch. By fighting in secret, fighting dirty, doing undemocratic things, we keep this infection controlled. We make the world safe for democracy. Does that sort of make sense?"

Still Chris said nothing; but this time it was because he wanted to hear more. He nodded.

"No, it's not easy, this kind of work," Fletcher said. "It isn't clean. You can't expect to feel good about it. But we're feeling bad on behalf of all those people out there, the innocent ones. We're not innocent; we *know*. I don't know if you're religious. The Garden of Eden—you know that story? The tree of knowledge of good and evil. Remember that? Before you eat the fruit you're innocent, whatever you

141

do is innocent, because you don't understand. Then you eat it. And you're never innocent again. You *know* now. And that's painful; it's a terrible thing. I know what I'm asking you, Chris. I'm asking you to betray a man you thought was a friend. I'm asking you to taste the fruit.

"But I'll tell you something. Losing that innocence is the first step on the road to *real* knowledge. To wisdom, if you like. You can't get wisdom till you lose that innocence . . . . Those people out there — innocent, because they don't know. Like children. Like sheep. No sheep can do evil, because it's innocent, right? But no sheep can do good, either. If you don't know what it is, you can't do it. So it's paradoxical, isn't it? You can't do good unless you stop being innocent. All the real good in the world is done by people who've tasted the fruit of that tree. And found it bitter and painful, just as you're finding it bitter and painful to betray Barry Miller.

"Well, there you are, Chris. I can't put it any clearer than that. We've come right down to the bedrock. I won't force you; I won't make you do anything you don't really *want* to. Don't make your mind up now. Think about it. What time d'you knock off work?"

"Five, half past, depends what there is to do." Chris's voice sounded far away even to himself.

"Okay. Fine. Don't give me an answer now. Can you come and see me again when you knock off?"

Chris nodded. Then he said, "No. I'll tell you now. You got a piece of paper?"

Fletcher leaned across, took a notebook from the glove compartment, and opened it to a blank page. He handed it to Chris together with a ball-point pen.

There was a sick, excited feeling in the pit of Chris's stomach as he carefully drew a sketch map of the junction on the Woodstock Road, the road down to Wolvercote, the canal, the track through the woods. He took his time; it was important to get it right. Then he turned the page and sketched the group of huts.

"That's great," said Fletcher. "Superb. The next question is, when does he go there? If I knew he was going to be there at a particular time, I could arrange to have him arrested. We can surround the place. He'll be armed. Far better to do it there than somewhere in town or at his house where he can keep his wife and child hostage. . . . Any idea when he's likely to go to this place?"

There was a roaring in Chris's ears.

"I can get him there tonight," he said. "I was going to finish off a job for him. I can phone him, arrange for him to come there."

"Brilliant," said Fletcher. "Magnificent. But please, Chris, *don't* go there yourself. It'll be dangerous. Say to him that you'll meet him there at—let me see, how long will it take to get organized? Ten o'clock should see everything in place. Is that too late? I mean, will that sound odd to him? You know, put him off?"

"I shouldn't think so. I'll tell him I'm going to finish the job at ten o'clock tonight, and can he come and check it. He might say no, it's too late, or he might be busy. Or he might just not want to come. I can't *make* him come."

"'Course you can't. Don't worry about that. Say that to him, anyway. But *don't* go there yourself. Let him walk into the trap. Okay?"

Chris nodded. He couldn't speak.

"How's the time now? You'd better not be late back; they'll want to know where you've been."

His hands curiously light and alien, Chris put the half-eaten apple into his lunch box and set Fletcher's bottle of mineral water on the carpeted floor of the car. He felt privileged and full of fear. He felt as if Fletcher were the guardian of some high secret, like a priest at a shrine, and Chris was being initiated into the mysteries. It was the feeling he'd touched the edge of when he'd argued with Mike Fairfax—this sense of absolute truths, of great powers with names like honor and justice. He felt a spring of gratitude gush brightly in his heart.

"Yes," he said to Fletcher. "I'll do it."

"Where's Barry?" he said to Tony an hour later. "Isn't he coming in?"

"He's in the shop all day. Some problem with the accounts, I don't know. Probably fiddling the sales tax."

Chris went into the office and telephoned the shop.

"Hello, Barry? It's Chris."

"Hello, Chris, what's the problem?"

"No problem. I was just calling about the shed. I've got

144

one section of plasterboard to finish and make good. I thought I'd do it tonight."

"Fine. You've done a great job, Chris."

"Listen, Barry, d'you think you could look in later on? About ten?"

"Why?"

"'Cause I want to show you an idea I had. It'll be ready about then."

"Actually, I'm going out this evening. Playing squash in Abingdon, then I'm seeing this bloke. . . . No, hang on, come to think of it, that'll be fine. I'll have finished by then. I'll look in on the way home. Okay?"

"Great. See you later."

"Ta-ta, Chris. You're doing a good job."

thirteen

Chris was wrong in thinking that Jenny hadn't seen him when she came out of the shed with Barry. She had, but it had been like seeing a ghost. He seemed to be there only for a split second, and the surprise was so great, coming just after she'd been thinking of him, that she could scarcely breathe; but it was enough to register the anger, the grief, the loss in his expression before he turned away. A moment before, that surge of unexplained happiness, like a blessing; and now, like a curse, this apparition.

She said nothing about it to Barry. He was full of his own preoccupations. Besides, she thought, he was too cheerful to understand.

Next morning he took her to the shed, as they'd arranged, stopping to buy some more plastic curtain rods, enough for all the windows, and some ready-made curtains. Later in the day, he said, he'd bring over some paint. She found she enjoyed the quiet of the woods; she'd been afraid that she'd find it oppressive, but she felt safe among the sunny trees, surrounded by the secret innocent life of birds and insects. At lunchtime (a can of beer from the fridge, a packet of potato chips, a bar of chocolate) she found her way down to the canal, and was surprised beyond measure to see not only a heron, which she recognized, but also a small brown animal swimming along by the bank and nosing its way into a tunnel. There was a whole world here. How strange not to have noticed it until so late!

That afternoon Barry came back with the paint and brushes, and she set about painting the plasterboard. He was right about its needing several coats; the paint sank at once into the porous surface. Still, it dried quickly.

When he came to fetch her home, he said, "That last bit of plasterboard'll be done by tomorrow. Oh, before I forget, how are you fixed for tonight, baby-sitting?"

"Okay," she said. "I'm not doing anything else."

"Sue's got this evening class. Normally I'm at home meself, but I'm going down to Abingdon to see this bloke about scenery. They're doing a play down there and they've hired some of our stuff, and I've got an idea about a much bigger range. There's a fantastic market, Jenny. Unbelievable demand. Not just plays and stuff, dramatic societies. We can help people think big as far as, you know, parties, weddings, discos. . . . Why not have a party on the moon, eh? Or a disco on the Grand Canal in Venice? The sky's the limit! Ready-painted scenery, lights, atmosphere, the lot.

Bugger just bopping about under a strobe light or a glitter ball; unleash the imagination! We could have a full range, all ready to put up! And. . .and marquees, lanterns, effects—you name it. . . ."

As he drove her home he elaborated further, until the whole world seemed to be crying out for him to cover it in canvas and fantasy, while he got effortlessly richer and richer as his imagination burgeoned.

Barry had already left when Jenny arrived at his house to baby-sit. Sean was in the bath, and Jenny sat in the kitchen talking to Sue.

"Barry was telling me about his idea for scenery," she said.

Sue rolled her eyes upward. "Can you see anyone paying a lot of money to get married in a mock-up of Red Square or the Grand Canyon?" she said. "I don't know, I think he's daft sometimes."

"Maybe not get married, but it might be fun at a party," Jenny said. "Depends how much it costs. But I suppose there's plenty of people with money." She was thinking of Piers and his friends, though somehow she didn't see that sort of person paying for that sort of thing.

"Well," said Sue. "He seems to be doing all right—I mean financially, you know, the business. I thought it'd be touch and go when we came down here, but he seems to keep making money. I suppose I can't complain."

"I should be so lucky."

"Yeah." Sue laughed. "Right."

"Where are you going tonight? In case, you know. . ."

"Ah. There's an evening class at the Poly. I shouldn't, really; I should concentrate on the O.U. work, but it sort of rounds it out. The number's on the memo board by the phone."

"What's the class about?"

"Nineteenth-century women novelists. Honestly, Jenny, I feel like *Educating Rita*, I'm just learning so much; the world's getting bigger all the time."

"Do they have classes on animals and birds and insects and stuff like that?"

"Bound to. Here's the catalog." She pulled a pamphlet from a shelf above the fridge.

"And can anyone go?"

"Anyone at all. There's just so much to learn! I'll go and chase Sean out of the bath."

While Sue was upstairs, Jenny looked through the pamphlet. It was true: there was an enormous amount to learn, and if you actually wanted to, and could choose what you wanted. . . She remembered Chris's urging her to get some A Levels and go to university. There might be a way there after all.

"How's the shed getting on?" said Sue, coming in to gather up her books before leaving. "Oh, I know about it, don't be surprised. I'm not supposed to've seen it yet, so I don't know where it is. But you know Barry, he can't keep a secret."

"Oh, it's. . .I've been painting. . . . There's a bit of wall still to finish." Did Sue know about the man Carson, or not? Did she think the shed was just a place in the woods? Jenny was thrown off-balance, so she hardly heard what Sue said next.

"Chris is going to finish that tonight, Barry says. He's going to look in there and see later, so I'll probably be home before he is. Sean's getting ready for bed. He takes forever; I don't know how he manages to spin it out. You okay, then? Coffee, milk—"

"Sorry," said Jenny. "Did you say Chris?"

"Chris, yeah, nice boy. He's working for Barry over the holiday."

"Is he—" Jenny could hardly speak. "Is he tall, with thick, sort of dark blond hair?"

"Yes. And shy. Good-looking. D'you know him?"

"Yes. I think so. If it's the same one. I met him and— and then we lost touch because I didn't know his surname or where he lived, and I had to leave the place I was living in. . . . Oh, God, I can't hardly believe it."

Sue was looking at her curiously, or compassionately, or as if she was happy for her; but Jenny knew Sue's mind was on the class, so she stood up and pushed the car keys into her hand.

"Go on, you'll be late!"

"Jenny, what is it? You're crying—"

"I'm not! Honest!"

"Well, what is it, then, love?"

"I just thought I'd never see him again, and suddenly. . ." She shrugged, smiling, wiping her eyes. "I sort of imagined it. I sort of pictured. . .but I didn't really think. . . Oh, go on, I'm fine. You'll be late; don't miss your class."

Reluctant, intrigued, Sue opened the door to leave, but then remembered something else.

"Oh! I don't know, life's too complicated. Listen, if the phone rings, leave it, don't answer it. Barry's bought an answering machine. Just let that take care of it. I don't know, men and their toys. . . . See you later."

Jenny waved from the doorway as the yellow Metro turned the corner. Then she went back inside, closed the door, and, clapping her hands, gave a little involuntary jump of triumph. But almost at once the look on Chris's face came back to her. He'd seen her coming out of the shed with Barry. He couldn't have thought. . . She blushed to the roots of her hair.

Still, he was going to be there working in the shed that very evening. And Barry would know his address. She could reach him. She could explain everything. It would be all right.

Sean called from upstairs. She tried to clear her mind for the chess game he was bound to ask for, and got up. Her face kept breaking into a smile.

Chris couldn't stop trembling. When he got home his mother asked him if he felt all right, was he getting the flu? He snapped an answer and thirty seconds later could no longer remember what he'd said to her. Mike Fairfax was reading the paper at the kitchen table with a pained expression. Suddenly Chris couldn't bear his home anymore.

"I'm going out," he said. "I'm going to see Dad."

He said that because he knew it would affect them. In fact, he didn't want to see anyone. He checked his bicycle tires and went out to ride around the highway, hard, head down, till he reached Hinksey Hill in the south, where he turned off and climbed till his muscles burned and his lungs felt raw. But the hill wasn't big enough. He needed mountains. He rode along the mile or so toward Boars Hill, down the other side, then turned around and drove hard at the slope again. Back and forth he rode, six times altogether, till the ache in his muscles was genuinely uncomfortable; and then he threw himself into the long descent of Hinksey Hill, the curving sweep down between trees with glimpses of the city in the late evening sunlight, and out into the big junction that straddled the main highway to Abingdon and the south. He didn't touch the brakes once, but it wasn't recklessness—it was despair.

And nothing happened. The traffic was quiet. The bike freewheeled out of the junction, slowing down gradually, coming to a halt by the Volkswagen dealer's next to the Park-and-Ride. The evening was calm and warm; it seemed to belong not to Oxford at all but to somewhere more southern, Mediterranean, and to another time.

Chris wished he were in that somewhere else, or any other place where things were simpler.

As he rode wearily toward the city, he realized that he hadn't once thought of Jenny since lunchtime. Maybe that was part of the price that Fletcher had spoken about.

It was getting dark as he reached the city center, just after nine o'clock. The place was thronged with foreign students, moving between the pubs and the hamburger joints, or simply drifting about in bored groups, smoking, staring. Chris cycled slowly down Broad Street, past the lit-up windows of the bookshops and the bleak stone bulk of the Bodleian Library on the corner, and turned up to the left, toward home.

But someone called his name from the pub across the road. There were people sitting on the pavement or standing outside with their glasses of beer; there was a crowd inside, visible through the glowing window. Who was it?

"Chris!" It was Dave, calling from the doorway.

Chris got off his bike and walked it across the road. Dave was with a group of half a dozen others, and he looked as they did: happy and slightly drunk.

"Wotcher," said Chris, glad to have a reason not to go home.

"Have a drink. What you going to have?"

Chris wasn't old enough to drink alcohol in pubs, but he looked it. He accepted a pint of lager and sat down with them, slightly curious to see the friends of someone he knew from work. He hadn't spoken to Dave much since the fight with Piers; the occasion hadn't arisen. But he liked him, and it was pleasant enough to sit here on the warm

153

pavement, with music coming out of the pub behind him and the throng of young men and women all around.

One of the girls said to him, "Are you the person who had a fight at the Oxford Union?"

Chris was glad it was getting dark, because the question made him blush.

"Yeah. I think I must be. Does it show or something?"

"No! Dave told us. Incredible. Molly, listen. This is the guy who had that fight, you remember?"

"Oh, right!" another girl said, looking at him as if he were a celebrity. "Wow!"

Chris looked at Dave, who raised his glass, grinning.

"Today the Oxford Union, tomorrow Caesar's Palace," he said.

"Who were you fighting?" said the first girl. "What was it about?"

"It was pure animal fury," said Dave, before Chris could reply. "There was no reason for it. This boy's nature, ladies and gentlemen, is untamed and savage. He has the instincts of the panther combined with the strength of the giant anthropoid ape. Unprovoked, he is docility itself; but if you transgress the law of the jungle, he will leap at you in the twinkling of an eye, a snarling, clawing mass of steely muscle—"

"Oh, piss off, Dave," said the second girl. "Just 'cause *you're* too much of a wimp to get into a fight. . ."

"I'm his *manager!* I'm not a wimp! I've got a really big cigar, look—somewhere—"

While the others were laughing at Dave, the first girl said quietly, "Sorry. I didn't mean to embarrass you."

She was pretty. He would have liked to talk to her, but the time for that was past.

"It's all right," he said. "I suppose it was funny, really. I just made a mistake."

"What, you thought you were fighting someone else?"

"Something like that. I've forgotten myself. I don't always go around having fights."

"I don't think I've ever seen a fight," she said. "Not a real one. I don't mean boxing matches."

"Didn't they have fights at your school?"

"I went to a terribly, *terribly* posh girls' school. We weren't allowed to have fights. Daddy wouldn't have paid the colossal bill if we came home covered in black eyes and scabs and things. The most we could do was cut each other to pieces with our razorlike sarcasm."

"Useful gift to have," Chris said. "I can never think of the right thing to say till about a week later."

"So you swing your fists. Take no notice of Dave, by the way. He's drunk."

Dave himself said the same thing twenty minutes later, when Chris looked up to see him, bleary-eyed, standing a foot or so away.

"Look, Christopher," he said carefully and clearly. "I want to apologize for discussing your private sorrows with this bunch of wastrels and strumpets. The fact is, I'm as drunk as a fish. It's my birthday. Did I tell you that? Not many people can say 'wastrels' and 'strumpets' on their birthdays. I mean, when they're drunk. So I—what was I saying?"

"About me and that stupid fight. But look, forget it, for God's sake."

"Of course. It's already forgotten. What's forgotten? I don't know, I've forgotten."

"Yeah, look, I've got to go. Thanks for the drink. Happy birthday."

"Oh, don't go, don't go. Did you have a nice time with the man in the car, the white Mercedes? What's his name? Carson."

Everything stood still. For a moment or two there was perfect silence. Then Chris felt his knees buckle, and he clutched at Dave for support.

"What did you say?" he heard himself whisper. "His name—what was it?"

"Carson," said Dave. "He was hanging around yesterday looking for Barry. He said he was an accountant. I thought he was chasing him for taxes or something. I told him for a joke that Barry was probably in his hideout. So he said, 'Where's that? I'll go and give him a surprise.' I said I didn't know. I said he should ask you. 'Chris is the boy you want,' I said. 'Chris'll tell you . . .'"

Chris couldn't hear any more. He felt as if he were being burned at the stake: the roar of flames, a terrible weakness all along his limbs. . . . What was the time? He shoved his way inside to look at the clock on the wall, through the cigarette smoke. It said half past nine. And Fletcher—Carson—had said ten, get him there by ten. Chris had never felt so helpless.

The first girl, whose name he still didn't know, said, "Are you all right? What's the matter?"

"I've got to find a phone. Is there a phone in here? Oh *Christ*, I haven't got any money—"

"I've got a phone card," she said. "Borrow that if you'd like. Here, let me help; you don't look as if—"

The two of them were close together in the crowded, smoky bar, surrounded by young men and women all shouting to hear each other. Dave and the rest of his party were outside. Chris tried to pull himself together.

"Listen, can you do something for me? Can you make a phone call? I've just heard something from Dave—I've got to go and head someone off. It's desperate. Can you make this phone call?"

"Yeah, 'course. Just tell me—"

She had a pencil in her bag. Chris wrote down the number.

"I don't know who'll be there. It'll be his wife probably. Doesn't matter—just say Carson's on his way to the shed right now—for God's sake keep away from it. Got that?"

"For God's sake keep away from the shed, because Carson's on his way there right now. That it?"

"That's it, yeah—"

"Hang on! Wait! Who am I calling? What's his name?"

"Miller. Barry Miller. I've got to run. . . ."

157

As he shoved his way out through the crowd on the pavement, the girl watched him, puzzled, and turned to look for a telephone.

Jenny had played chess with Sean and lost. She had asked him about the little animal she'd seen by the river, and he'd told her it was probably a vole or a water rat; he'd even found a picture of one in his encyclopedia. And while he was having a last ten minutes' reading time, she took the volume down to the kitchen to look through while she had her coffee.

All the time, underlying everything she did and thought and felt, was the knowledge that Chris was there, there in the shed, there now, at this moment, and that soon Sue would be home, and she could borrow Sue's bike and go there before Barry got back, and find Chris, and everything would be restored.

The feeling was so strong, the prospect of happiness so certain, that she didn't hesitate this time to hug Sean and kiss him when she said good night. It was just fondness. It was safe to be fond of anyone now.

As she was pouring the boiling water into her coffee mug the phone rang. She jumped and hurried into the hall, where the phone was, only to remember that Sue had told her not to answer it. She got to it just as the answering machine came on. She'd never seen one before, and she stopped to watch curiously as the cassette clicked on and a girl's voice spoke.

"Oh, God, I hate these things. Listen, I've got a message for someone named Barry Miller, okay—hang on—"

There was a lot of noise in the background. It sounded as if the caller were at a party. She went on: "Sorry. Someone's buggering about. The message was: Carson's on his way to the shed right now. Don't go there, for God's sake. I think that was it. I'm sorry, I don't know his name, the guy who asked me to phone. He was in a rush. Okay? That's it. Bye."

The phone was put down at the other end, and after a few seconds the cassette stopped revolving.

One part of Jenny's mind was thinking: so that's how an answering machine works. The other part was filled with a hideous image of a body hanging on a hook with its throat cut: the grotesque fate of the gang members in the story Barry had told her: the death Carson had dealt out to his rivals.

And Chris was there in the shed.

"Oh, God," she said quietly, looking up the stairs to the lighted landing and Sean's half-open door. She couldn't leave him; she was being trusted to look after him. But surely Sue would be back before long, and meanwhile . . .

She tore herself away from the hall and ran into the kitchen. Should she leave a note? It would take too long. In the little narrow carport, next to a wheelbarrow and a Black & Decker Workmate and a lot of Sean's clutter, stood Sue's bicycle. Less than a minute after the phone had first rung, Jenny was riding hard along the road to Oxford, standing up, pounding the pedals.

As he drew closer to his own home Chris slowed down. What was he doing? Where was he going? He'd been fooled, easily and completely fooled by someone who knew exactly what arguments he'd listen to. He'd never dreamed he was so stupid, so naive. But what was he going to *do* about it?

He stopped and pulled the bike onto the pavement, wheeling it along as he tried to sort out the terrible confusion his thoughts were in.

First, how true did he think Barry's story was? Was Carson, or Fletcher, really likely to kill him? Impossible to answer. He'd heard both men; one of them must have been lying. But did Fletcher, or Carson, seem like a killer? Or did Barry seem like a terrorist? Everything looked equally shadowy and unlikely and askew.

And second, insistently: What was he going to *do* about it? Chase up there on the bike . . . and then what? Shouldn't he call the police?

He was at the corner of his road. Only a hundred yards away was his house, and his mother, and Mike; and although Mike was a wimp, he wasn't a fool. Chris had never needed someone's good advice so much.

He left his bike beside the back door and went in. The kitchen was dark, but the television was on in the living room. He paused in the hall, unsure, and then went back to the phone in the kitchen. At least he could ring Barry's number to make sure that girl had given the message.

The phone rang twice, and there came the click of an answering machine. His heart fell.

"Hello. Barry Miller speaking. I'm not home at the moment, but—"

Then the line was interrupted. A woman's voice, distracted, said, "Hello? Who's that? Is that Barry?"

He didn't know who it was, because she sounded so frightened, but then he recognized Sue's voice.

"No, it's me, Chris. Listen, is Barry—"

"Where are you? Where's Barry? What's going on?"

"Did she ring up with my message? That girl?"

"Yes—about Carson. Oh, Christ, I've just come home, and Jenny's not here. She must've—"

"*Jenny?*"

"She was baby-sitting—"

"But, what the hell—Jenny?"

"She must've heard the message and—oh, God, Barry must've told her about Carson, and she knew you were in the shed. That's where she—"

"I'm not! I haven't been there! I've just found out about Carson and. . . What do you mean about Jenny?"

"She was here. She didn't know about you, that you'd been helping Barry. She was so happy when I told her; she thought you were in the shed tonight finishing that wall, because that's what Barry told me, and when I told her she was like a kid with a Christmas present. I couldn't believe it—she was so happy she was crying, poor kid. Oh *God*, she must have heard the message on the tape and gone there to warn you! Oh, Jesus, help us! I thought this was all over, Chris. That *fucking* Carson and his brothers—I wish they

161

were all damned in the pit of hell. . . . And where's *Barry?* He's going to go there in ten minutes. What can I *do?*"

Chris found himself saying, "Call the police. I'll go and look for Barry. Head him off."

Sue had been crying, but Chris couldn't comfort her. Jenny was there. It hadn't been true about her and Barry. And Carson was on his way to the shed.

Chris ran for the back door just as his mother came into the kitchen.

"Chris! What's going on? What's all the panic?"

He tried to speak, but found himself helplessly shrugging, and then he ran out to his bike and flung himself on, riding like a demon.

Five minutes later he was at the entrance to the track through the woods. It was too rough to ride on; he thrust his bike into the bushes before setting off on foot.

After a few yards the track turned off to the left, and the glow from the streetlight on the road behind was soon swallowed by shadows. Only the moon shone now. Chris half walked, half ran along the rutted, potholed track, raising clouds of dust from the dry surface. The bewildering tangle of shadows, the inconstant silver and the deceptive black, brought back Jenny's presence more strongly than anything else since they'd last seen each other; it was just like the light among the trees by the lake on the night they'd met.

He stopped to catch his breath; his muscles, after the punishing ride earlier on, were protesting.

"Jenny," he said under his breath. "Jenny!"

Somewhere nearby a bird was singing in the darkness, trills and carolings of immortal richness. He thought that Jenny might be near enough to hear it too. If he called out. . .

He took a breath, but held it, as something gripped his heart.

The most extraordinary sound was coming from behind him on the track, a sort of low, growling, crunching noise, as if from some hideous animal.

He turned, clutching the nearest tree trunk, and saw it.

It was pale and huge. Like a blind slug it was nosing its way along the track, crushing the stones, shouldering aside branches and nettles, slick-skinned, blanched, hideous. He nearly fainted with fear. Only when it had passed did he see it for what it was: the white Mercedes with its lights out, its engine barely purring. He felt the sickness of horrible fear giving way to shame, then to a greater fear again. And then it had gone past and out of sight, and that vile, all-devouring crunch of tires on loose stone was already muffled.

He ran forward after it. The clearing wasn't far. If he shouted she'd hear him, but he was afraid; he was so lapped about with fear that he could hardly breathe. He thought: Carson won't kill her; he'll see it's a girl, and he won't do anything to her. As soon as he sees who it is. . .

He saw the pallid gleam of the car through the trees ahead. It stood at the edge of the clearing, lights still out, and when he came up to it he saw that the driver's door was open. There was no one inside. Everything was in darkness, including the shed.

The light!

Barry's crazy, complicated system—they still hadn't fitted the infrared detector, and *she might not have been able to find the switch—*

Suddenly he cried, "Jenny!" with all the force in his body, and at the same moment there was the crash of a gun, appallingly loud.

It smashed into the silence six times, making his ears ring, as birds flew up in alarm and the whole night seemed to shriek.

Chris was clutching the door of the car. A figure came out of the dark shed and walked steadily toward him. It seemed to bring with it waves of pure evil, like cold air flowing out of the open door of a freezer. Chris's heart quailed; he heard himself whimper. Fletcher—Carson— stopped at the hood of the car and struck a match. The little flare, held at the level of his chest, illuminated his face like hellfire. His expression wasn't human. Chris shrank away in pure speechless terror.

"I advised you to stay away, Chris," Carson whispered. "It's no fit place for an innocent person. This is the pit of hell. No one destroys my brothers. That's unpardonable, to do that to a family. Especially mine. You see, I'm a demon, me. I'm a killer. I'm the angel of death."

His fathomless eyes looked into Chris's soul until the match burned out. Then he got into the car and unhurriedly started the engine. He backed out into the narrow track before driving silently back into the dark.

Moonlight drenched the clearing. The windows of the shed were blinded by curtains, and the door stood open. Chris, nearly fainting with fear, was conscious only of a sort of hideous grandeur. The twisted columns of the trees, the heavy canopy overhead, and, above all, the silence of that open door awed him. Carson had been right to whisper. Chris felt that if only he could remain still and quiet, he could hold the very worst at bay. He hardly dared to breathe.

Then, not from Wolvercote but from the other direction, he heard the sound of a different engine and saw headlights flickering among the trees. He hadn't realized there was another way into the woods. Chris wanted to wrap the darkness around himself and hide, but it was too late, for the van had reached the clearing and stopped. The light on the trees was sharp and terrible.

Barry Miller, in a yellow polo shirt and white shorts, his hair rumpled, got out and called cheerfully, "Wotcher, Chris! Given up, had you? I got held up in the pub. Here, listen, I got a surprise for you. We're gonna. . . What is it? What's the matter?"

In the flat glare of the van's headlights the shed looked more frightening than anything else in the world. With a cry, Chris stumbled toward that appalling open door.

He reached it just before Barry did, feeling his way in, fumbling down by the electricity meter for the switch.

165

When the light blazed on, he had to shade his eyes because it was so bright, and there was so much blood.

Jenny lay on the bed. She had pulled the duvet over herself, and only her feet were visible, one tucked over the other. She was lying on her side facing the wall. She hadn't died at once, despite the number of bullets that had hit her, because she'd had time to write something on the freshly painted wall with a finger dipped in her own blood. It was smeared and shaky, but unmistakable: DAD.

"He never. . ." whispered Barry. "Carson? But why. . ."

"The light," said Chris, in someone else's voice. "She didn't know where the switch was. In the dark, he couldn't tell—"

"Oh, Christ."

"Go and get the police," Chris told him.

Barry swallowed, nodded, turned. Then he said, "Is she. . .you sure she's. . ."

"Police, doctor, everything. Just call nine-nine-nine."

"Yeah. Yeah."

Chris waited, clinging to the door, till the lights of the van had disappeared among the trees. Then he turned off the light with a trembling hand and sat on the bed beside Jenny. He had so much to tell her, but the horror overcame him and he shrank away from her, from that dear body he'd loved so much. And betrayed.

Then he knew what he had to do next. His gorge rose, and he nearly vomited; cold sweat broke out on his face, but he controlled himself. There was no choice. He had to make amends. On the table there was the Swiss army knife. The sharpness of the blade was very clear to him, and the weight of it in his hand, and the rightness, the correctness of what he had to do. He opened it and lifted it twice, but each time his courage failed, and the nausea in his throat changed to sobbing, so that when they arrived and found him there, they thought he was crying for Jenny.

fourteen

They never found Carson. Two days after Jenny's death, the police discovered the white Mercedes in a parking lot at Heathrow Airport. If he had left the country, he hadn't done so under his own name; he might have gone anywhere in the world.

Inevitably, the truth about the stolen money came out. There was hardly any of it left. Barry had used some of it to buy the business, and most of the rest to subsidize it, since Oxford Entertainment Systems was making a steady loss. Sue's feeling of unease had been well founded. She'd believed Barry when he'd told her that he didn't know where the money had gone, that the Carsons must have been hiding it all this time. The shock of finding that her husband was a liar and a thief, and that their lives had been built on sand, was hard to bear. Barry was sentenced to six years in prison. Sue and Sean left the house in Kidlington; Chris didn't

168

know where they went, because he never saw them again.

During the weeks and months that followed, Chris's life lay frozen in a tundra of shame. In his solitude, he often thought about what Carson had said to him as they sat in the white Mercedes, about innocence, about good and evil. It was very strange. Carson had appealed to the highest part of him, not the lowest, and although the wisdom he spoke came from the tongue of a liar, still it was the truest wisdom Chris had ever heard. He knew he'd be living with it for a long time to come, perhaps for a lifetime, until it became part of his own self. He might never find anything truer.

He had acquired another kind of wisdom, too. In that moment in the shed, he'd seen something that few people ever see: the limits of his own nature. Unlike anyone around him, he knew precisely how stupid he was, how easily fooled; precisely how much he feared pain; precisely how contemptible he was; that at a time like that he could cry for himself but not for Jenny. Knowledge like that was rare. It put a mark on you. He'd be hard to fool again.

As for Jenny, there was an inquest. Her parents were traced, and Chris watched them as they sat, numb, in court, their pinched faces elderly and drained. No one could understand the significance of the word that their daughter had written on the wall, and the coroner, sympathetically, didn't press the point. Had she tried to say that her father had killed her? Had she mistaken Carson for her father? Was she trying to leave a message for him? It was impossible to know.

But Chris had his own idea. It came to him when he saw

Jenny's father cover his face in court. At that moment Chris found tears coming to his own eyes and knew they were tears for Jenny at last; and he saw the meaning of the message she'd wanted to leave. She had loved her father and wanted him there in her last moments; she was calling for help. Chris understood. He was glad she'd been able to do that; he probably would have done the same himself; it was how a family should be. And that was a comfort to him.

Philip Pullman is the author of the highly
acclaimed Sally Lockhart trilogy: **The Ruby in the
Smoke,** winner of the IRA Children's Book Award
for Older Readers, **Shadow in the North**, and **The
Tiger in the Well**. All three titles were named
ALA Best Books for Young Adults. His other
books include **The Broken Bridge**, a novel set in
present-day Wales, and **Spring-Heeled Jack**, a
comic thriller. A former schoolteacher, he lives
with his family in Oxford, England.